Green Tree

M.L. Hendry

Green Tree

To my parents, Russell and Rebecca

In loving memory of Marjorie Lynn

Copyright © 2025 Matthew Hendry

ISBN: 978-1-7640382-2-5

Cover and rune art designed by Travis Ibbotson

***

First Edition

The Shadow Runes

 Shade

 Beam

 Wave

 Height

 Kinetic

The Life Runes

 Protect

 Call

 Grow

 Devine

 See

Green Tree

Chapter One

The arrow soared past, piercing its target dead on. The victim gave a screech and dropped where it stood. The bowman looked pleased as he looked upon his foe. The deer before him looked up at its assailant and almost seemed to beg him for mercy. The bowman withdrew a hunting knife and quickly ended the deer's life.

"Fantastic hunting, Josh," came the voice of the bowman's instructor.

Watching from a distance, Andrew Saran approached. He was proud of his apprentice. He was already one of the most skilled Cadets of the Royal Protectors of Harleland. Ever since they had returned from the quest to the Great Tower of Hoonth almost two months ago, Josh's archery skills had continued to grow and grow and grow.

"Mrs Crakanthorpe will appreciate this," said Josh. "And it's big enough even for my father to sell some of the meat in his stalls!"

"It's a great catch," replied Drew. "Maybe its antlers will make nice decorations, too!"

"The biggest challenge now will be to haul it back to the orphanage!" Josh pointed out. "Do you think your friend Hermit could give us a hand?"

Drew shrugged. "Probably, if I asked him. But then again, it's an hour's ride back to Dempair, which is a long way to go just to deliver a message and come straight back!"

Josh laughed. "Sounds like you're just lazy!"

"Sounds like you're disrespecting your mentor!" retorted Drew with a smirk. "But in all seriousness, I can't leave you out here on your own. The Greenarch Plain is crawling with the Herk soldiers of the Crownlands."

"I can fend for myself now!" pleaded Josh. "You said it yourself - that you think I'm better combat trained then you were when you left for Hoonth!"

Drew looked at his steadfast apprentice in annoyance. "If an entire patrol of Herks ambushed you out here you'd be done for," he said. "We shall have to lug that deer back by ourselves."

Josh nodded. Together, master and apprentice hauled the massive catch up onto Josh's horse, the steed grunting as it felt the weight upon its back.

"Right," said Drew. "Ride with me Josh, I don't think Busteed will be able to carry you *and* the world's biggest deer."

"Good boy," Josh whispered to his horse. Busteed whinnied and gave Josh a lick on the face. The young Cadet joined Drew on his own steed and they set off, climbing the slopes of the Dirtgula Mountains as they travelled closer to Lekt Valley, home of the village of Dempair. They rode at a steady pace, Busteed the horse keeping up behind them, attached to a lead held by Josh who sat behind Drew. Drew thought back to his return to the orphanage weeks prior. It had been a sunny day when Drew, Josh and Geetie Gunnersbury, alongside their other friends Tenebrae and

Octavia, arrived at the orphanage in Dempair. Phil Fisher
had been left dumbfounded by Geetie's offer to purchase the
orphanage that he and his wife Julia had operated for many
years. There was no hesitation in the former orphanage
master accepting Geetie's offer, and soon both he and Julia
were gone, to where, no one knew. Although he had found
Phil pleasant enough, if grouchy, Tenebrae's abuse suffered
under his watch was enough to make him end any sort of
relationship he had previously had with his foster parents. It
had come to his attention that it had been Julia who insisted
on the mediaeval punishments Tenebrae and others had
suffered. Drew had never liked Julia, and since Geetie had
taken over as the new orphanage master, the place had
improved. Children were happier, the place seemed better
maintained, and things just all around seemed much livelier
and more soulful then they did under Phil and Julia. He
smiled. When he and Josh returned home from their hunt,
they could catch up with Geetie and Hermit. He hoped that
Geetie would have his Lyre with him, allowing for the
singing of many songs. But there was still underlying
anxieties gnawing at him. Those being the state of his
Kingdom. When he and his friends had finally arrived at the
Great Tower, the mythical fortress in the land of Hoonth far
to the north, the great Ker Gorûn had decreed that the raging
and bloody Civil War between Harleland and its Dutchy of
the Crownlands must cease. For nearly twenty-two years, the
war had raged, thousands on both sides had died, and yet
both King Lakton of Harleland and Duke Shârvous of the
Crownlands had continued the hostilities. Over the past
months, the Crownlands had successfully cut off the main
supply routes between the Greenarch Plain and Dirtgula and
the Harlelish capital, Boron Nigh. An alternative supply
route via the treacherous Sea of Many Currents had been

arranged, whereby merchant vessels from the Port of Dirtgula navigated shallow seas, stormy weather and the white waters of a most hostile kind. This was enough to ensure the populations of Boron Nigh, Dempair and the town of Hogs to the west of the capital where fed, however strict rations had been implemented.

It was why this deer Drew and Josh had caught was so important, and many other Protectors across the land had been sent on similar hunting missions to gather more food.

It had taken a little over an hour and a half at their slower pace when they finally arrived into Dempair. The orphanage, the village's biggest building, loomed on the left of the main street, while the bull yard, operated by the bull herders, was on the right. Waiting for them by the entrance of the orphanage was Geetie.

"Ho, friends!" he called. His eyes widened when he saw the deer. "Well now!" he said in surprise. "That is quite the catch!"

Josh dropped down from Drew's horse, as his father assisted him in taking the deer from Busteed's back.

"This will feed the whole orphanage for a week!" exclaimed Geetie.

"Lord knows we need it, too," said Drew, joining them. "Those rations are barely enough to fill even half of our daily calories." He looked at his apprentice. "Come on Josh, we'll tie up our horses and deliver the deer to Mrs Crakanthorpe."

Josh nodded in agreement, and they led their steeds toward the stables.

***

"You gonna save some bread for me?" That was the mischievous voice of Hermit.

Drew looked sadly at the remaining slice of toast before them. He had already eaten his slice, and his stomach had nearly convinced him to go for Hermit's.

"The sooner these rations can end the better," said Drew.

"I know," replied Hermit. "King Lakton has to do what he thinks is right." He laughed. "Since you've been back from Hoonth, I think *I've* become the patriotic one!"

The two friends shared the remainder of their lacklustre meal together. Drew shuddered as he again felt the chill. Winter was well and truly setting in in Harleland, and for a Kingdom that already had food rations, the season did not help the gathering of food. The deer that Drew and Josh had caught earlier that day was hard enough to find, and Drew sighed as he realised they would have to undertake the same hunt everyday for the rest of the season if they were to properly feed their people.

"What did you say that old woman's name was again – the one who gave you the cloaks, I mean?" asked Hermit, shivering.

"Ern," replied Drew. He laughed. "Honestly Hermit, I've told you the story of the quest that many times, but it's like it goes in one ear and out the other!"

Hermit ignored his insult. "Well, tell me again then! And this time tell it in a way that *doesn't* make me immediately forget everything!" he snickered.

Drew sighed outwardly, but internally he did enjoy recounting the tale. Once more, as had happened various times over the past few weeks, Drew recalled his journey to the Great Tower to Hermit. The challenge of Cold Valley, the marshes of Dirtgula, the storms of the Sea of the Sun... And Tenebrae. Indeed, as promised, they were still together even after the quest had ended. Although they were unsure of what they were, Drew knew he at least wanted her in his life, even if they were just friends. Meanwhile, Drew and Octavia had helped to run the resistance against the Uprising movement from the orphanage.

The Uprising movement, Drew thought with bitterness.

If the Crownlands was not bad enough, this god-for-saken cult-like group was a whole other story. Taking advantage of Harleland's weakened state after years of war, political opportunists had tried to take over the Kingdom from the inside.

His mind wandered to Octavia. The wise old Protector, who had once been the Chief of the Protectors. He had been stripped of his title by King Lakton, the Lord of Harleland furious that he had accompanied Drew the entire way to Hoonth. Or perhaps it was a way for the King to take out his anger after Ker Gorûn refused a military alliance. He told

Hermit once more of the betrayal of Duke Ritticüs Czmith of Dirtgula, of how they sheltered with Ern in the Outer Dirtgulas as they crossed the sea, and of the Voksenkollen Tribe, a vicious tribe of wildmen from the Northlands. Of King Zinton of Wiln. And finally, of the Great Tower. Yes. The Great Tower of Hoonth. Hermit gasped as Drew told him once more of the revelation that the tower's ruler, Ker Gorûn, was actually his long lost grandfather, Jonnothŏn Saran. The Ker's message, the entire point of Drew's quest, had been to end the war, for Harleland and the Crownlands to find peace. The company returned home with this message, desperate to make King Lakton listen. They made quite the entrance on the back of Kora, the Dragon of Hoonth who was named after Drew's first love. But despite everything, it was to no avail. Kora had vanished, to where no one knew, and now domestic affairs in Harleland were not in a good state.

There was also a great sense of loss for Drew. Before he left Harleland, the first girl he had ever loved had been cruelly cut down by a Herk of the Crownlands. The loss of Kora had turned his hatred of the Crownlands into an obsession with their destruction. His every waking thought had been consumed with thoughts and dreams of plunging a dagger deep into the heart of Duke Shârvous. However, he had mellowed out over the course of his quest thanks to his friendships with Josh and Tenebrae, and the guidance of Geetie and Octavia. Even when his mother, San, sacrificed herself for him in the Great Tower, he withstood the temptation to barge headstrong into the Black Fortress of the Crownlands to murder Shârvous, an event that would have certainly resulted in Drew's death before he had even crossed the Dutchy border.

There was one more thing. The runes. The mysterious magic stones crafted from a mythical ley line that passed beneath the Great Tower. But Drew did not want to share that. The runes were currently safe in their bag, kept securely within Drew's cloak. They were *his*. And he enjoyed their power.

"And now," said Hermit, following Drew's recount and snapping him back into reality. "That Uprising movement Inquisitor, Count Balnather, has sent some of his loyal Protectors to directly control each village of the land, placing restrictions on the general population and taking all tax revenue for himself and the top of Boron Nigh."

Drew shook his head at this news.

"A small band of rebel Protectors had attempted to unionise against him, but they have all been imprisoned for mutiny, from what I heard," continued Hermit. "The movements of King Lakton and Prince Lekt are also heavily surveyed by the Uprising movement."

"Probably an attempt to prevent the royals from addressing growing rebellions across the country," called Geetie from up the table, listening in to Drew and Hermit's conversation.

Drew felt anger rise in him at this news. Hermit had also told Drew of other happenings, including the appointment of Dempair's Regional Administrator, Marlo. She had been appointed by Balnather to enforce the Inquisitors' rule over Dempair, and she often greeted Drew with displeasure whenever she came to the orphanage for inspections. The political corruption within Harleland worried Drew, and he wondered again what he would do to stop the war and fulfil Gorûn's wish.

"All is not well in Wilder Forest," Octavia said.

Drew listened intently to his friend, dread coursing through him as they sat with Josh, Geetie, Tenebrae and Hermit in the orphanage office. Since Phil's departure, Geetie had rearranged the entire room, unblocking the window behind his desk and filling the bookshelves with novels, as well as cook and music books.

"More Herk attacks?" Drew asked.

"Always," replied Octavia, speaking in a tone that said 'obviously.' "But also… I have heard rumours of dissatisfaction coming from the higher ups in that Dutchy."

"So Herks *and* the Uprising movement?" asked Josh.

Octavia frowned. "Herks yes, but I don't think the Uprising movement has a foothold there. I think it's dissatisfaction borne out of what is transpiring in Boron Nigh."

Tenebrae shook her head. "How have things become like this?" she asked.

"They were bad before we left for Hoonth, but not like this," said Josh.

"I think the problems were there," replied Octavia. "I don't think I realised how much control Balnather and the other Uprising Inquisitors had until after Lakton removed me as Chief Protector. And it wasn't until we came back that the

Uprising movement sent Marlo out here to Dempair to monitor things."

"Octavia, it's been weeks," Drew began. "And we are still no closer to stopping the war. I mean, we can't even get a meeting with King Lakton's *messengers*." He sighed. There was one other idea he had. A dangerous one. One that had festered in his thoughts for several weeks. But as he opened his mouth to make his suggestion, Octavia cut him off.

"Oh dear," said the old Protector. "The stalker is coming." He said the second half of his sentence with venom.

He stared out the window, and sure enough Drew saw Marlo walking across the lawn.

Geetie sighed. "I shall go down and greet her," he said reluctantly.

"Allow me," said Tenebrae. "I'll complain her ear off. Make sure she never comes back." She smirked.

Josh laughed. "Well, that *would* do the trick!"

"Oh, stop it you two," said Geetie as he went to leave the office. "I'll be back soon! …hopefully."

Drew grinned. Josh and Tenebrae continued to banter, while Hermit and Octavia had seemed to move onto a conversation about moles.

"Trust me my young lad," said Octavia. "A mole is easily caught through stealth! I once caught five in one hunt! I just set my bow and arrow up and *bang!* Five tasty moles for dinner!"

"I guess I'll take that on board," replied Hermit. "I just prefer the method of reaching down their holes and catching them that way."

"Octavia, no need to give these *animals* any time of the day," a voice sneered. The five friends looked toward the doorway in displeasure. It was Marlo. "Look at all these orphans behind these bars. I almost pity them," she continued.

She laughed as she walked over to Drew. She ignored the others.

"I have a message," she began. "From Count Balnather."

Drew curled his lip. "What does he want?" he asked.

"He said that he wishes to meet with you tomorrow evening," she said. "You are to see him in the Palace of Merthru. He wishes to talk to you about a new job."

Drew looked at her confused. "New job?" he asked. "What job?"

Marlo snickered. "That's for you to find out," she said. "I'm not sure why our gracious Lord wants a filthy orphan like you to work in the new administration, but if I were you, I'd be honoured. Leave at first light! Do not be late!" She looked now at the others. "Josh Gunnersbury," she snickered. "How is Saran's training? Low quality I imagine!" She turned to Tenebrae. "I'm surprised nothing has gone missing around here with a *thief* living at the orphanage now!" And her insults continued, chiding Hermit for his injuries whilst fighting the Herk soldiers who had killed Kora after their invasion of the orphanage before Drew had left on the quest to the Great Tower. She insulted Octavia for his demotion. And as she walked out, Marlo could not help but insult Drew one last time.

"How does it feel to be stuck back *here* again after your little quest?" she asked. She whipped around and stormed off, yelling at Geetie to show her out.

"Yes ma'am," replied Geetie, although Drew could tell in his voice how much his friend hated calling her 'ma'am.'

A collective sigh of relief went up from all present once Marlo was gone.

"What a piece of work she is," said Tenebrae.

Josh nodded in agreement. "Where does the Uprising movement find these people?" he asked. "Balnather and Marlo are both as weasley as each other!"

But Drew felt great levels of anticipation. "Why in the world would Balnather offer me a job?" he asked.

"This is our chance, Drew!" said Octavia excitedly as he got to his feet. "To get back into the circles of power! To finally have a genuine shot of changing things around here!" He collected his things. "I must set off for Boron Nigh at once!" Octavia declared. "I must speak to Naz…"

Naz, the young Protector whom Drew had met when he first went to Boron Nigh before the quest, was stationed at Palace Rock in the top part of the city. Octavia met with him on the same day every week at midnight to exchange information.

"I shall meet you there," continued Octavia. "I shall await you at the East Bay Protector Unit tomorrow night after you speak with Balnather."

With that, Octavia strode out.

"Marlo never said anything about you needing to go alone," said Josh. "Octavia could have at least given you a lift!"

"He's going to a secret meeting, Josh," replied Drew. "It's better we go separately... In saying that, you're right, Marlo didn't say anything about me needing to go alone."

"Looks like we're going to Boron Nigh," said Josh with excitement.

Tenebrae looked at Josh. "Which means an early start tomorrow," she said. "So no sleeping in!" she finished with a laugh.

"What makes you think I sleep in?" asked Josh. "Do you watch me or something?"

"You wish!" Tenebrae replied.

"For the sanity of everyone here," began Hermit. "Please stop flirting. Please and thankyou."

Chaos ensued, and excuses and explanations rang out around Drew. But he was not thinking of Josh, Tenebrae and

Hermit. He was thinking of Balnather and this job. What was the job? Tomorrow he would find out.

Chapter Two

"At ease, soldier!"

Naz looked ahead at Renault. The new Chief of the
Protectors certainly had a new way of running things. In
Naz's opinion, they were certainly for the worst. Renault
was a tall, dark, and brooding figure, but he was certainly not
quiet when it came to giving orders. Naz shuddered as he
remembered the previous day's training session, when the
Protectors of Boron Nigh were forced to run up the slopes of
Mount Merthru. He had always been ambitious, Naz
remembered. Renault had always been one to question
Octavia's commands, and was always very close to a
wealthy Uprising Inquisitor named Hoop.

"Trevault," began Renault, looking at the muscular form of
the Protector on Naz's left, the Chief's brother no less.
"Remember your training. What do we do if a peasant has
broken curfew?"

Trevault looked straight ahead. "They are stripped of status,
sir," he replied.

A cruel smile appeared on Renault's face. Naz felt
uncomfortable. He had joined the Protectors to serve the
people of Harleland – not oppress them.

The Chief of the Protectors now looked in his direction.

"Young Naz," he began. "Octavia's prodigy." He sneered.
"Tell me. If a peasant is caught obstructing a Protector, what
do we do?"

Naz stared straight ahead. He did not look Renault in the eye.

"We…" he choked out the last words reluctantly. "Take them to the border."

The border.

He felt sick. Peasants that displeased the Uprising movement or their power tripping supporters were taken to the Greenarch Plain's Dutchy border with the Crownlands and left for dead. He could not fathom how such a cruel scheme had come to be tolerated in Harleland, but with Count Balnather on the Kingdom's council and wielding such influence, Naz could no longer be surprised by anything.

"Excellent," replied Renault. "The border. And where do we take Protectors who fail to follow their orders?"

He seemed to stare into Naz's very soul with the last part of his sentence.

He doesn't suspect that I'm up to something, right? Naz wondered. After all, what he was doing was not a complete betrayal of the new regime, right? As it so happened, Naz was giving his former Chief and now good friend Octavia inside information into the happenings of Palace Rock, the top of Boron Nigh. As he gazed around the square that the troop of Protectors stood in, he could see the Royal Palace standing proudly before him, with several high class houses surrounding them on all sides.

Naz gulped as he finally answered. "They must prove their loyalty by capturing… the Witch," he said.

For one reason or another, Count Balnather was obsessed with catching the Witch that lived in Cold Valley. Naz had heard from Octavia how the Witch had nearly tricked him, Drew and the rest of the Great Tower company as they passed through Cold Valley on their way to Hoonth. Some suspected that Balnather wanted to tame the Witch, giving him a powerful ally should any more rebellions against the Uprising movement's reign rise up. Some just thought he was outright mad. But those brainwashed few thought that he wanted her to join Harleland's Protectors to help defend against the Crownlands.

"That's right," said Renault. "Any Protector – any at all – who goes against the orders of me or our Lords the Inquisitors will be sent to the Cold Valley to capture the Witch." He looked across the assembled troop.

"You will all be up at first light tomorrow," he announced. "You will meet back here in the Square. And failure to do so will see you spend tomorrow night with the *peasants*." He spat the last word with contempt. "Dismissed!"

At that, Naz hurried quickly back to his quarters. It was time to conduct his weekly update for Octavia. And tonight, he had big news. News that concerned Prince Lekt, son of Lakton and heir to the throne of Harleland.

Naz and Octavia met in a secret location behind the Palace, at midnight once every week. Since the Uprising movement had blocked off the sewage pipe between the top and bottom halves of the city, Octavia had been forced to find another way to the top half. Stunningly, he had been helped by a crew of former bandits led by a man named Cron, who had tried to rob Drew when he had first come to Boron Nigh months before. They had found a disused trail that went from the bottom half of the city and up Mount Merthru, before coming to a large tree that must have fallen into the city wall years ago. Octavia was able to climb up the trunk and over the wall of the top half of the city, emerging in a seldom patrolled alleyway behind the Royal Palace.

"What news my friend?" asked Octavia, sweating from the effort of climbing up the tree and over the wall. "I apologise for my lateness – I came as quick as I could from Dempair."

Anticipation flowed through Naz. "Well…" he began. "Prince Lekt has vanished."

Octavia looked at Naz wide eyed. "What?" he asked. "Where? When?"

"Two days ago," replied Naz. "King Lakton is saying that his son just upped and left without telling him. But I suspect he's saying that to throw the Inquisitors off."

"Then we must find out where Prince Lekt is and if King Lakton has sent him somewhere," Octavia replied. "And I have some news of my own."

The former Chief of the Protectors explained to Naz Balnather's message to Drew.

"I shall meet with him tomorrow to find out what this job of his will be," Octavia finished.

"These are interesting tidings," replied Naz. "Hopefully things can start to turn in our favour. Renault is still sending 'misbehaving' Protectors to Cold Valley."

Octavia shook his head. "I went to that valley recently to see if I could intercept the lot he sent last week… I was too late."

Naz's jaw dropped. "Y-you mean…" he stammered. "That Jerzaun, and Lilthyme are… dead?"

Octavia nodded sadly. "Yes, my boy," he said. "I'm afraid so."

Naz felt anger pulse through him. He hated Balnather and what he and his fellow dictator Inquisitors were doing to the people of the land he loved.

"So what's the plan now?" he asked.

"Well, I think we need to find Prince Lekt," replied Octavia. "I shall send Tenebrae to search for him. She and Josh are accompanying Drew here tomorrow. Josh's training has come along remarkably well also. He is making a fine Protector, as is Drew."

"That is good to hear then," said Naz. "Good news in a bad time."

"Indeed," replied Octavia. "He is nearly fifteen, so young, yet has a long and fruitful career ahead."

Naz allowed himself to smile. But the weight of the situation bore down upon him again.

"I will be back this time next week," continued Octavia. "Good luck, and I'm sorry, but you must keep up the façade." He paused. "We will get you out of here Naz."

Naz nodded, and Octavia turned, climbing the wall and vanishing from sight. Naz could do nothing but hold his breath and pray as he stood alone in the dimly lit alleyway behind the Royal Palace, his mind filled with a mix of determination and fear. The weight of his double life as a Protector and a spy for Octavia's underground resistance was becoming heavier with each passing day. The atrocities committed by the Uprising movement and their loyalists, and the consistent invasions of the Crownlands, had pushed Naz to the brink of his conscience.

He knew that the time for action was approaching. He wondered what Drew's new job would be. Would it help them to overthrow the Uprising movement and finally force a peace meeting between Lakton and Shârvous? Naz clenched his fists, steeling himself for the challenges that lay ahead.

As he made his way back to his quarters, Naz couldn't shake off the image of Balnather's sadistic smile, and the cruel man Renault who enforced the Uprising movement's rule. The thought of innocent peasants being subjected to the ruthless punishments imposed by the new regime fuelled his determination to bring about justice. He vowed to protect the people of Harleland and restore the honour and integrity of the Protectors.

I just hope that Octavia comes back as usual next week, he thought. It was imperative that he knew what was going on in the outside world if the plans he had thought over a million times in his head would come to fruition. Plans to mobilise the Protectors still loyal to the Crown and the common folk of Boron Nigh against their new masters.

As he entered his quarters, a small room shared with several other Protectors, which made his living conditions unbearably crowded, he heard the dreaded sound of Renault's voice behind him.

"Soldier!" it demanded.

With the knowledge of the importance of his façade of loyalty, Naz reluctantly turned to face his commander.

"Yes, sir?" he asked.

"I want to congratulate you!" said Renault.

"Congratulate?" answered Naz, confused. "Why would that be, sir?"

"On your appointment to the next battalion of *brave* Protectors that shall set out to capture the Witch, of course!"

Naz's heart sunk.

No, he thought. This would ruin everything!

"You leave at first light!" declared Renault. His face did not give away his emotions, and Naz could hardly see through the gloom. With that, Renault marched away, back toward his personal chambers near the Palace. Naz's shoulders drooped as he headed into his quarters and lay down on his bunk. Sleep did not come quickly.

Chapter Three

Drew's annoyance was palpable. He seethed with anger as he faced the Protector standing before him, Marlo gazing at Drew disdainfully.

"I am sure I can get to Boron Nigh myself, thanks!" Drew exclaimed, his voice dripping with anger.

"And how do I know that you won't just run off?" Marlo asked. "If one of my Inquisitors wishes to see you, then see him you shall."

Josh went to say something but was silenced by a look from Tenebrae.

"So I can take my apprentice to the Greenarch Plain for training, but I can't escort myself to Boron Nigh?"

Marlo sneered. "You can do exactly what *I* allow!" she replied.

The night before had been sleepless for Drew. Anticipation had consumed him as he awaited his return to Boron Nigh to discover what this supposed job offer from Count Balnather entailed. However, Marlo had now insisted on escorting him directly to the city.

"Come on," sneered the Protector. "We haven't got all day!"

Begrudgingly, Drew followed Dempair's Administrator out of the orphanage, Josh and Tenebrae in their wake. Geetie and Hermit watched on from the orphanage, its master deciding to stay behind to watch over the orphans. Sourness coursed through Drew as he looked ahead of him at Marlo and reflected on his situation.

"She's so pleasant, isn't she?" said Tenebrae.

"Oh yes," replied Drew in the most sarcastic tone he could. "Delightful."

The four now galloped upon their horses up the side of Lekt Valley. Memories returned to Drew of when had first made the journey to Boron Nigh. As they passed the clearing where he had been attacked by Brigmington and a patrol of Herks, he had haunting memories flood back. His mood soured even more. The journey was relatively uneventful as the four arrived into Boron Nigh after nearly a day's ride. The city's side entrance looked slightly different from the last time Drew was there. The Uprising movement's crest was plastered on the gate, and new Protectors that Drew had never seen stood guarding the entrance. They looked at him with unpleasant eyes.

"Make way you oafs," Marlo spat. It seemed her disrespect did not stop at just Drew but anyone unfortunate enough to get in her way. The Protectors shuffled to the sides of the gate hurriedly and unbarred the entrance.

Perks of power I guess, he thought to himself as the Protectors glowered after them.

They rode through the city and up to the upper walls of Boron Nigh, riding up the great staircase to Palace Rock, where they dismounted and a groom attended their steeds.

"What does Balnather want from me?" Drew had asked once again. Marlo had ignored all of his earlier attempts at conversation during the ride and he decided she was going to answer him now once and for all.

"Can't you listen?" She sneered. "His excellence wants to give you a job! Although I can't imagine what good you'd be for any position other than fodder for the border." He ignored her provocations. He could not wait to be away from this old hag. Secretly he hoped that Balnather would give him a job in a higher rank than her. He was aware of her droning on in the background, but chose not to listen.

"...If you had nothing to hide, you would have nothing to fear!" she finished haughtily. Marlo looked at him in anger when she realised Drew had not been listening. "Hey! I was talking to you!" she screeched.

"Oh I'm sorry," replied Drew. "I just heard this really *annoying* sound coming from your mouth – I didn't realise they were words."

She grimaced at him, went to spit some nasty insult, but gave up on finding one that would appropriately detail her hatred of him.

"Good one, Drew," said Tenebrae with a smirk.

Drew, Josh, Tenebrae and Marlo approached the great castle walls and Drew was once again taken aback by the size. A single stone in the wall was the size of his entire torso and yet the castle was made of thousands of them. The halls of Boron Nigh had changed for the worse. Once it was adorned with the faces of old kings and ancestors. Great heroes of the

Merthru dynasty and bygone eras were replaced with dry drab nothingness. Even the fine carpet that lined the floors had been torn up to reveal the plain stonework underneath. Marlo remained silent as she led him through the depressing halls. He imagined that the Inquisitors had removed the culture and history of this once hallowed hall entirely to demoralise King Lakton.

The atmosphere was tense with an air of hostility as more Protectors passed them in the halls. Drew saw a few familiar faces but overall, he was disappointed to see all emblazoned with the Uprising movement's crest. By the time they reached the large double doors leading into the Great Chamber, Drew was positively drained. Marlo barked at the two Protectors standing guard to open the doors and grant them access to see Balnather.

"Ma'am, the Inquisitors are in a meeting with the old king Lakton at the moment," a young Protector apologised.

"The *old* king will have to wait." Marlo snarled. "He'll have to find out one day that he doesn't hold the privilege of his old rank!" She was obviously relishing the power she held in this new system, and it made Drew sick to his stomach.

"Yes of course ma'am," the Protector acquiesced. He opened the large doors with his silent partner and announced the presence of both Marlo and Drew to those within, his voice echoing off the walls. Lakton was looking furious and seemed to be in the middle of a vicious tirade before the doors opened, cutting him short. Balnather looked pleased with the distraction and upon seeing who it was entering his hall he smiled all the wider.

Marlo blocked Josh and Tenebrae from entering behind Drew. "You two shall await us out here," she said.

"But–" started Josh.

"No buts, boy!" she replied.

Marlo turned and followed Drew inside as Josh and Tenebrae cursed.

"We shall continue this discussion at a later date," Balnather said to Lakton as Drew and Marlo approached.

"You will do well to listen to my warning Balnather, there will be hell to pay if you–"

"*You are dismissed*," he said again, a touch petulantly.

Lakton stormed down the steps that lead up to one of the three new wooden thrones Balnather now sat in. Beside him sat the other Inquisitors of the Uprising movement who Drew did not recognise. The hall had once been a beautiful Kingly chamber, with advisors stationed around the throne when King Lakton still had his full powers, but now Drew saw Balnather and the other Inquisitors sitting alone on their thrones. The sharing of power outside the Inquisitors had all been an act and evidently they had found ways to remove all other voices within the castle but their own and the King.

"My friend!" Balnather greeted Drew warmly, his thin lips curling into a smile. "I see you have met the talented Marlo. She is quite the administrator you know." Marlo gave a polite bow at the mention of her name and nudged Drew forward.

"Great Leader, I present to you Andrew Saran, of Dempair! As requested he has been transferred from the orphanage directly into your charge!" Marlo proclaimed, obviously enjoying the sound of her own voice and the sole attention of one of the de facto leaders of Harleland.

"Very good Marlo, you are dismissed," Balnather replied with a careless wave of his hand. She bristled slightly at Drew's side but gave another polite bow.

"As you wish, Great Leader."

She was quickly ushered out of the hall by another Protector, leaving Drew alone with the three Inquisitors. Balnather continued to look at him for a moment longer before speaking.

"Allow me to introduce Count Mossjoint, one of my fellow Inquisitors of the Uprising movement," he said. "Once he was the Count of Canterbury, the capital of the Greenarch Plain, before it was destroyed and annexed by the Crownlands, no thanks to Lakton."

Mossjoint, a small and unpleasant looking man, looked upon Drew in annoyance.

To his right, Balnather introduced the third Inquisitor. "And this is Count Hoop, the Count of the West Bay of Boron Nigh."

Hoop appeared like the rest of the Inquisitors, certainly unpleasant and somebody that Drew wanted nothing to do with.

"He seems like a commoner to me, Balnather," said Mossjoint. "Men of our stature need not trade words with someone like him."

"Of course, Mossjoint," replied Balnather. "However, as much as I am displeased to say it, his travels through Harleland, through Wiln, all the way to Hoonth, are what we need."

"Meaning?" asked Hoop.

Balnather looked at his fellow Inquisitors with a sinister look, before turning to Drew. "Prince Lekt is missing!" he declared. "Petty King Lakton has refused to tell me of his whereabouts. He claims that Lekt has just upped and left without telling him!"

"A fat bunch of malarkey that is!" sneered Mossjoint.

"I wish for you to report back to me *any* information about Lekt's whereabouts." His unpleasant eyes beamed. "And then I want you to arrest him and bring him back here to stand trial. You're a Protector – and I am ordering you to execute a warrant." He nodded at Hoop who descended from his throne and handed Drew a piece of parchment. It was indeed a warrant for the arrest of Prince Lekt, on charges of treason.

"The rewards for you, Mr Saran, will be great," Balnather finished.

Drew narrowed his eyes. "Will I be permitted company?" he asked. Quickly, as Balnather opened his mouth, Drew added:

"Lakton did not permit me company on my previous quest – you don't want to be like him, do you Balnather?"

Balnather scowled. "You can bring one companion," he declared, although he did not seem particularly pleased.

Drew knew he was only allowing it to come across as different to King Lakton.

Weak fool, thought Drew.

"Now go, Saran!" called Balnather. "Find Lekt and bring him to me *alive*. Failure to do so…" He paused. "Will result in a penalty of death."

Chapter Four

The following day arrived, and Naz joined the assembled troops in the square. He exchanged glances with Trevault, who shared his disillusionment with the current state of affairs, despite his brother's command. They both understood the significance of their roles in the upcoming events. Naz looked around at the other Protectors that had been assembled. He was shocked to notice Jemima, a young warrior around his age that Naz had watched climb through the ranks over the past several months. She looked shyly in his direction, causing Naz to blush and turn away in embarrassment.

Count Balnather's booming voice echoed across the square and distracted Naz from thinking about Jemima, the so-called 'Inquisitor' of the Uprising movement reiterating the orders for the mission to capture the Witch in Cold Valley, Head Chief Renault by his side. Naz felt a surge of anger at the thought of exploiting the legendary figure for the Uprising movement's selfish gain. The Witch was a symbol of fear in Harleland, grave tales of her wrath told over generations. He remembered back to what Octavia had told him about the time he and Drew had encountered the Witch as they had passed through Cold Valley. Naz shuddered as he imagined being subjected to the same torturous visions that the Witch had conjured for Octavia, Drew and the others. She had been left alone in that valley for several years, and Naz believed it was the best that it remained that way.

Dismissed from the gathering, Naz hastened back to his quarters with one last glance at Jemima. Trying to cast her out of his mind, he instead tried to distract himself with thoughts of an impending revolution. Naz just hoped that whatever Drew's new job was would help the cause.

And perhaps Prince Lekt, too, he thought, the heir's disappearance still causing Naz to ask many questions.

He remembered earlier that morning, before the sun had risen. While the others slept, Naz had quickly pulled out a small, worn notebook from underneath his old and tatty mattress. The notebook was a lockable journal, and only those with the key could read its contents. He and Octavia had decided upon hiding this journal in a secluded location should anything unexpected occur between their meetings, with one key each being held by both Protectors.

Naz sat at the small wooden desk in the corner of the quarters, lit only by the dim glow of a single candle. His mind was a whirlwind of thoughts, but he forced himself to focus. Carefully, he began to write.

'Octavia,

The Uprising movement is moving faster than anticipated. Balnather and Renault have ordered a mission to capture the Witch in Cold Valley, of which I am to be deployed.

Remember what you told me about the visions. We cannot let her fall into their hands.

I am to leave at first light the day after our last meeting · I need your guidance and the support of our group ·

We must be united now more than ever ·

Naz "

He finished the message and locked the journal. Quickly, he exited the room and began to walk toward the secret meeting place that he and Octavia exchanged news at each week. Naz knew he needed to be cautious. The top of Palace Rock was constantly watched, and he knew he would be in heavy amounts of trouble if he were to be found breaking the night curfew for off duty Protectors.

All was well however as Naz slipped into the dark alleyway behind the Palace of Merthru and quickly climbed the damaged wall. He used the fallen tree on the other side to carefully climb down. He stood now outside of his occupied city of Boron Nigh. He placed the journal beneath the tree, in the exact spot agreed upon by himself and Octavia. Then, he climbed back over the wall and returned swiftly and quietly to his quarters, near the old sewer building that Drew and the Great Tower company had used to climb to the top of Palace Rock almost two months before. He breathed a sigh of relief. At least Octavia would know of his fate. He was not sure if he would survive Cold Valley.

Back in the present, Naz rode at a steady pace behind the chosen group of the Cold Valley mission. Speeding up slightly so he could ride beside Trevault, he pondered a question that had been formulating in his mind since being appointed to this task, but heavy surveillance had prevented him from talking with his friend.

"Do you think they suspect we're up to something?" Naz asked.

Trevault shrugged. "Maybe," he replied. "They know that both of us disagree with their methods at the very least. And they know that you're extremely close with Octavia."

Naz was still unsure whether to share with Trevault that he had been meeting with Octavia in secret. He decided it would be for the best not too. As his mentor had said, it was impossible to trust anyone at the moment.

"I mean this task is a punishment for dissenters," continued Trevault as they continued to ride forward, by this point reaching the exit gate to the city. "Yet this mission feels... different. I mean Count Balnather himself addressed us, and a Sergeant is also leading us." He paused. "I think it may be a legitimate attempt to capture the Witch this time."

"Okay, so *half* punishment then," Naz said with a smirk.

Trevault smiled. "I suppose so," he said.

Naz felt sorry for his friend. His own brother was the cruel new Chief of the Protectors following Octavia's firing, and yet Renault never gave Trevault any acknowledgement. It was like Renault had forgotten his sibling was related to him. Naz slowed his pace and allowed Trevault to go on ahead, but to his dismay he noticed Jemima ride up next to his friend. A small twinge of jealously coursed through him, but he tried to push it back down. The group travelled on in silence, leaving Boron Nigh far behind, not stopping until after nightfall.

***

Usually, a horse travelling at full pelt could reach Cold Valley from Boron Nigh within a day. But with the main road now controlled by the Crownlands, and that Dutchy's fearsome Herk soldiers patrolling the majority of the Greenarch Plain, the company were forced to take the lesser trodden side roads which wound their way around the base of the Dirtgula Mountains. This route would take several days, and there was still the likelihood of running into a band of Herks on patrol. As the sun set on the second day of the journey, Sergeant Elias, appointed as the leader of the mission by Chief Renault, ordered a halt.

"That will do us today, soldiers," he called. He indicated a small cave on the side of a nearby cliff. "That will be our shelter. Jemima. Kulu. Find us some firewood for the evening."

The two Protectors that Elias had indicated nodded and swept off into the darkening forest that surrounded them.

Elias was a decent Sergeant, and although Naz did not risk asking him of his genuine thoughts on the regime, he got the sense that his superior was not overly pleased with the current state of Harleland. Naz shook his head and walked up the rocky slope toward the cave entrance, Trevault and another Protector named Alfred in his stead.

"You have all done well so far," Elias started as the trio joined him in the night's shelter. "I have no doubt that when we arrive at the valley by the day after next, we can capture that Witch, for the glory of…" he trailed off, as if he were unsure who to dedicate his speech to. "…Harleland!"

Usually we dedicate ourselves to the King *and Harleland,* thought Naz.

He again had a wave of realisation pour through him, at just how dire things in his country truly were. The Uprising movement had taken control of the Kingdom, specifically the capital, while the Crownlands provided an outside assault. How had it come to an entire Dutchy *and* a peasant uprising hijacked by corrupt Counts laying waste to Harleland?

After a while, Jemima and Kulu returned, and Elias permitted a small fire so as not to arrest the attention of any Herks that may be patrolling nearby. Naz had heard stories of far too many Protectors being embroiled in scuffles with the Herks, the Crownlands own battalion of soldiers.

"Commander Warren told me I can be deployed to the frontlines against the Crownlands in a few weeks!" Jemima said excitedly, breaking Naz out of his thoughts.

He gulped. Would that mean he would not see her around anymore? Not that he cared, of course. Or at least that was what Naz tried to convince himself of.

"Good to hear, my girl!" replied Elias. "It will be better for *all* of us once we are back out there. This isn't *Sergeant*

Elias saying this, but I am over the dreadful politics of Boron Nigh."

"Aren't we all, sir," said Kulu. "Us Protectors should be out fighting the Crownlands, not watching over our own people, and *certainly* not our own King!"

Elias shook his head. "I must stop you there, young Kulu," he said. "As much as I have my own personal thoughts on Renault, it is still not the place for me or you to question his authority. He is still our Head Chief."

Kulu dropped her head and said nothing more. Her friend Jemima tried to restart the conversation.

"So, Sergeant, have you heard anything more from the frontlines?" she asked. "Is it true that the Crownlands may be after Hogs next?"

Elias shrugged. "That is what our intelligence shows. However I spoke to Octavia about it – I know he's not our Chief anymore, but he is still wise. He believes that a possible invasion of Hogs could be a smokescreen for a different assault." He paused. "However, Renault will not listen; in fact he refuses to even allow Octavia into Boron Nigh."

"He is permanently stationed in Dempair under the command of Marlo," said Naz.

At the mention of Marlo, a look of contempt came across Elias' face. "That old hag?" he said. "How she came to be a Protector is beyond me. Commander Blakshu believes her to have the worst attitude in any Protector she's ever seen."

"I'll tell you of one Protector with the *best* attitude," replied Naz, trying to lighten the subject, and to move away from talking about Octavia, lest he accidentally spill too much information. "Josh Gunnersbury, son of Geetie, is being trained by Andrew Saran – uh, so I heard," he added quickly. "Apparently, he is coming along extremely well – he could be battle ready by the time he's sixteen! Far earlier than any of us were."

Elias nodded. "Hmm, well that is good then. At least we have *some* good news, even if it is small."

"Sixteen?" asked Trevault. "Isn't that a bit young?"

"Well, he's nearly fifteen at the moment," answered Naz.

"That's worse!" replied Trevault.

"Oh, if he's fully trained I'm sure he'll be fine," said Naz. "The great Jenkins was apparently thirteen when he was made a full Protector, and I know that Octavia wouldn't allow Josh to be given that title until he is at least the same age as Drew – I mean, *Andrew* Saran is now." He stopped and repeated what he had said in his head. "I mean, I'm sure that *Renault* would not allow it."

Elias looked at Naz suspiciously. "You sure seem to know a lot about Octavia, and of these Josh and Andrew people," he said.

"Oh, I," Naz stammered. "I talk to a lot of the Protectors who come up to Palace Rock after coming back from the frontlines with the Crownlands."

"Hmm," said Elias, clearly not convinced. "Anyway, we must get off to sleep. Big day tomorrow. More riding!" He said the last part sarcastically as the Sergeant lay on his bedding and tried to go to sleep.

"Goodnight, Naz," said Jemima, smiling at him.

Naz's heart skipped a beat. She acknowledged him!

"Night!" answered Naz in surprise, giving her a weird toothy grin back.

He did not see Trevault roll his eyes.

I think they like each other, thought Naz sadly, that small twinge of jealousy coming back to him.

Yet he still smiled as he closed his eyes. For the first time in months, he realised he was thinking about things other than the Uprising movement. For the first time in months, he felt free.

Chapter Five

Drew was in a grouchy mood as he stared out the window at the rain covered streets of Boron Nigh. He yawned as he tried to make the effort to get the milk from the ice-box. The cold rain was still pouring down on the old wooden roof, like ice trying to penetrate a thick sheet of metal. Drew put the kettle on and grabbed some coffee beans from the small cupboard. This small apartment that Balnather had given him was certainly nothing like the much larger room he now had for himself back in Dempair at the orphanage, but he still appreciated the fact that he was at least able to enjoy some of the big city amenities that surrounded him. A few evenings before, he had accepted Balnather's 'job,' more like a task or even an order. Permitted only one companion, the trio of Drew, Josh and Tenebrae had formulated a plan. Soon, Drew and Josh would set out to find the missing Prince Lekt, while Tenebrae would appear to set off back to Dempair. Josh and Drew would journey to the village of Hogs, where they would rendezvous with Tenebrae in three days from now. Now, as Drew looked over at Josh, anxiety coursed through him, and that all too familiar voice in his head spoke again.

You could level *this city to the ground!* The voice told him. *You have the runes…*

Ah yes. The runes. The Shadow Runes to be precise. Drew had not used the runes since he returned from Hoonth. The violence he had committed the last time he wielded them could not be cast from his mind. He often had vivid flashbacks of when he combined the five Shadow Runes to form *Moarte*, a spell that brought death and destruction to the foes beneath him. He had killed two more Herks using the runes whilst in the Great Tower as well, and while he may not have cared as much should he have struck them with a regular weapon, the fact he used the runes made him uneasy.

You can never use those runes to kill – no matter who it is you kill, his mother, San, had told him.

He was unsure what effects his use of *Moarte* would have on him, along with his use of the runes to kill the two minions of the now dead Captain Dirk. However he knew enough from San, as well as from both Octavia and Gorûn, that he may have already started down a dark path. At the very least, the past few months had been good. Training Josh had been fun, and he enjoyed his friend and apprentice's company. He was certainly glad he was with him on this mission.

"I wonder where Prince Lekt has vanished to?" questioned Josh. "I mean, where do we even start?"

Drew shrugged. "We need to gather information," he said. "There's no saying where he's gone too. Balnather tried to get as much information out of King Lakton as he could, but to no avail."

He shook his head and made himself his cup of green leaf, sitting down by his small window and gazing out. The dirty white buildings of Boron Nigh seemed to stretch forever, only the blue-looking Dirtgula Mountains on the horizon confirming to Drew that the city actually ended. He also knew from his own travels that between Boron Nigh and the mountains lay the now dangerous and war torn Greenarch Plain. He sighed. It was a battle on two fronts, the innocent and valiant of Harleland squeezed by the Crownlands and the Uprising movement. And it seemed that King Lakton either had no power, or no motivation, to stop the corruption. He was certainly not motivated to speak to Duke Shârvous of the Crownlands. Drew felt anger rise in him. He still saw the Crownlands as a dangerous threat. Not only had they killed his first love, but one of Shârvous' vassals, Count Michael, Drew's uncle, had ordered the assassination of Drew's father. Then there was the malice displayed by Dirk, captain of the Crownlands' military. Although he had been defeated by Drew, Tenebrae, Josh and San back in the Great Tower, his lack of honour had resonated a strong message back to Drew. A reinforcement of how much he still despised the Crownlands, despite the many flaws of King Lakton. Finishing his green leaf, Drew readied himself to go out. He needed a distraction and decided that could be achieved via alcohol. He had finally turned eighteen the month prior and revelled in his ability to *legally* drink. He may or may not have drunk prior to his coming of age. Maybe one here or there. Or ten.

"I'm heading out," Drew declared, as Josh sat sipping the last of his own mug of green leaf.

"Don't tell me," started Josh. "The pub again? You went last night!"

"They had good beer!" Drew protested. He sighed. "I need to clear my head, Josh," he admitted.

"I know," said Josh in sympathy. "Just be careful. I saw the way you were clutching at the runes last night."

Drew narrowed his eyes suspiciously.

He's watching the runes, said the voice in Drew's head. *He's jealous of you.*

Drew made his way out the front door of the building, white limestone stained with dirt like the rest of Boron Nigh's structures. The rain had largely subsided but the coming night was still cold. He wrapped his coat around him, the very same bearskin cloak that Ern had given him and his friends back in the islands of the Outer Dirtgulas. He strode down the street, still busy and lively despite the glum times. Most people he walked past were poor and dishevelled, and he avoided eye contact with one larger man who seemed like he was looking for a neck to break as a way to take out his life frustrations. Eventually, Drew arrived at a local pub, a wooden sign hanging from above the entrance reading *The Sparkling Miracle*. A good name for a watering hole – Drew was looking for a miracle right now, and he decided it would come in pints. He entered the building and approached the bar. A skinny man was being served by the bartender and seemed to be swaying on his feet.

"Mate, I've only had two drinks!" the man was saying.

"Well it's two drinks too many," replied the bartender. "Now get out before I summon the Protectors."

"Aw, you're a dog mate!" complained the man as he stumbled away. He looked at Drew as he passed. "Oi, buy as a drink, ay?"

"Oh, uh," replied Drew. "I only have enough money for myself."

"Aw, that's what they all say," the skinny drunk complained as he made his way clumsily out of the pub.

"Sorry about that," said the bartender as Drew approached. "High time for drunks I s'pose." More quietly, he whispered. "The guy's a lightweight, wasn't lying about only having two drinks. And they were both mid strength! Ha!" He sniffed then stood up straight again. "Anyways, what can I get you?"

Drew glanced at the draught options. "A Hogshire Brew please," he said. "Pint."

"If you didn't order a pint, we'd laugh at you!" replied the bartender. "That'll be five shillings twenty-five thanks."

"Five twenty-five!" choked Drew. "I guess it's city prices around here."

Reluctantly, he forked out his money and paid the bartender.

"City prices?" echoed the bartender. "What, are you here from Hogs or something? I thought the Crownlands took control of the main highway out on the plains."

"Dempair," replied Drew. "Luckily the road to Lekt Valley is still open."

"Dempair!" said the bartender, surprised. "Well I never. Especially in these times. We never had too many folk from there come to the city. Low wages out that way I guess, probably can't afford it here."

"You're dead right," commented Drew as he looked at the beer that cost the same as the standard hourly wage back in his home village.

"There was one guy actually from Dempair who came in sometimes," said the bartender as Drew began to walk away. "His name was Brig."

Drew stopped.

"Oh, yes," stammered Drew as he turned back around. "The bull herder?"

"That's what he said he did!" said the bartender. "I always wondered why someone herding bulls in Dempair needed to have business meetings in a pub, but I never questioned it. Some of those people he used to meet were very shady." He stopped and looked around, then beckoned Drew to come back over to the bar. "Actually, some of those shady figures he met still come here sometimes."

Drew gasped.

"But I don't go questioning it, what with this Uprising movement going around telling us all what to do now," he continued.

Drew sat at a table by the fire with his beer and pondered. Brig was a Caller of the Crownlands, a position in their Herk battalions who was in essence a scout. He would call raids on both Dempair and surrounding farms and villages. Since his death, there had been significantly less attacks on Dempair. Was it possible, however, that these shady figures were also Callers or even other members of the Herks? He felt suddenly that Shârvous had eyes all around him. He felt suspicious of every single person who sat in this pub around him. He finished his drink and then promptly departed, wanting to return to the safety of his apartment. He had decided. He would leave tomorrow to find Lekt. Drew could no longer stand staying in Boron Nigh any longer. He knew he ought to report the suspicious individuals the bartender had told him about, but with the Uprising movement in charge, who knew whether they would take the report seriously or not. Drew sighed. He arrived home and prepared himself for bed, Josh already snoring soundly in the bed next to his, Drew hoping that a good night's rest would prepare him for his quest to find the Prince.

Chapter Six

It was noon on the fourth day and Naz and the other Protectors looked down into Cold Valley.

"I don't want to go in there," quivered Alfred.

"Unfortunately, you have no say in that matter," replied Sergeant Elias.

It was cold and misty in the vale. The whole time, Naz felt that he and the others were being watched.

"Ok," whispered Trevault. "How are we going to catch this Witch?"

"That's exactly what I was thinking," replied Naz.

They pondered this question as the company made their way down the slope of the valley. Trevault suggested a lasso, but Sergeant Elias laughed the idea off as tacky. Kulu believed they could draw the Witch out and then hold her down. Naz did not believe that would work for a second. Personally, he believed they would need to fight her and find a way to render the Witch unconscious. Only then could they take her back to Boron Nigh. Elias seemed to like his idea, and thus Naz's plan became the agreed upon tactic.

A slight drizzle came that afternoon as the Protectors rested in a slight dell in the rock. There were many stories that Naz's father Jed had told him of when he was young growing up on the coastline of Cernsland. The tale of Cold Valley was one of them. One day a young woman was crossing Dirtgula, passing through the old convict camps when she was seen by a group of rangers, strange men who patrolled the then un-owned lands between Wilder Forest, the Crownlands and Dirtgula. They pursued her, and as she tried to escape, she ran down into a large un-explored valley that lay just before the Gap of Dirtgula, a break in the mountain range where the modern day bridge crossing passed over Cold Valley and connected the Central Dutchies to Dirtgula. It was said from there on that she lived in the valley in a small hut deep within the gorge and practised witchcraft. Naz shuddered when he remembered his fathers' tales and wished they could all be done with this task. Elias had wanted to stand upon the top lip of the valley and get an idea of its outlay, however the heavy fog prevented it. As well as this heavy fog, there were eerie sounds coming from deeper in the mysterious valley.

Brunb, brum, bruin, they seemed to go.

"Well," said Elias. "Brave hearts everyone. Let's go."

The patrol rose and began to descend into Cold Valley. The sounds had been going on for some time, getting louder and more frequent the deeper into the valley they trekked. Naz felt that it was the Witch. And it appeared that some of the others seemed to share the same worry.

Jemima looked at him. "Is that… her?" she asked.

"I don't know," replied Naz. "Maybe it's just the fog. Maybe it's something else."

"It's her… it's the Witch for sure!" said a trembling Alfred.

"Oh, pull yourselves together!" ordered Elias. "We are Protectors of Harleland, Royal soldiers that should have no fear of this beast–"

Suddenly, the sounds started again, louder this time. Fear came over the face of Elias.

"Well," he continued. "We are brave! Ignore these noises. Kulu! Alfred! With me. We shall try again to get a view of the valley."

The duo that Elias selected followed the Sergeant up the slope and walked back up the valley. After a few minutes they stopped, almost halfway between where the others waited and the top. They had turned and were looking back over the valley. Suddenly, Jemima screamed. Trevault whipped around and gave a shout. Naz too felt it. A dark presence. So dreadful that he too shouted in fear. He realised that the grey mist further down the valley had darkened and began to swirl.

Was it her, the Witch of Cold Valley? If it was, would they be able to capture her?

How will we catch her and take her to Count Balnather? Naz thought.

"Don't worry," said a rather relieving voice, one that Naz could not believe he was hearing.

He turned to see Octavia. Shock coursed through him. How had he come here?

"Octavia!" cried Trevault. "Why?! How?!"

"Never mind that!" called Octavia. "You need to get out of here! Quick! Before the Witch gets you. She is coming."

At his words, the swirling dark mist turned black as ash, and he saw fire extruding from it. A loud cackle could be heard. The world became loud.

"Run!" commanded Octavia. "Forget Balnather's mission!"

At his orders, Naz ran, Jemima beside him. They ran up the slope, towards the exit to the valley. But then he stopped. Trevault! His friend was not with them.

"Jemima, where is he!" asked Naz.

"H-he was right there with me!" she replied.

They turned and looked down the valley. Octavia was gone! And Trevault's unconscious body could be seen being swallowed up by the black, fiery mist. Elias and the others clearly had not heard anything from above, as no help came.

"We must go back for him!" yelled Naz about the harsh noise. "And Octavia!"

"Naz, isn't it obvious?" Jemima called back. "That wasn't Octavia. I think it was one of the Witch's visions. There would be no way he could have come all the way out here for us, no way he could have known we went on this mission at all!"

"You don't know him like I do!" cried Naz. "Now, either help me rescue them, or get back up the top and stay out of my way!"

Jemima looked at Naz in horror. "Maybe *you're* the Witch vision," she said crossly, before making her way back up the slope.

I don't need her anyway! thought Naz, but he shocked himself at how harsh he sounded.

He quickly and carefully ran down the slope toward the resting place where Trevault had been absorbed by the mist. The noise and the dark fog had both begun to subside and to his relief he realised that he now had a decent view down the valley, nearly to the bottom. It seemed muddy down there, and he remembered that the bottom of the pit was a bottomless marsh, according to Octavia. Slowly, he made his way down, careful not to slip over on the dewy surface. The rocks and moss around him became even more slippery the further down he went. After a few minutes, Naz reached the bottom. Brown mud for as far as the eye could see reached off into the mist. How had Drew, Octavia and the Great Tower company possibly crossed this?

He paused to catch his breath, his eyes scanning the vast expanse of foggy marsh. He tried to take a step forward but his foot sank into the mud down to his knee.

"Great," he muttered.

The mud sucked at his boot, and it felt like it was pulling him in. Naz felt panic stir within him as he tried to pull his left leg out, whilst he knelt on the solid ground with his right knee. Finally, after almost a minute, the young Protector freed his left leg from the brown muck with a disgusting slurping sound. But his relief did not last long, as a strange voice spoke, seeming to come from all around him. Naz froze in fear.

"Naz…" the voice said.

He shuddered and looked around. "Hello?" he called. "Who's there? Is that you, Witch?"

Silence.

"Trevault! Octavia!"

More silence.

"Naz!" came the voice again, this time with more urgency.

"Show yourself!" screamed Naz.

"I grow concerned about the activities of Harleland, Naz," said the ghostly voice again.

"Please," said Naz, tears streaming down his face.

The horrible fear and feelings of his incoming demise had destroyed him. He dropped to his knees and dropped his sword beside him.

"I swear," he cried. "I swear I'm not with the Uprising movement. I don't want to capture you. Please believe me."

"Naz!" said a voice once more.

This voice, though, was different. Naz opened his eyes and saw the familiar shape of Jerzuan, one of the Protectors sent to his death in this foul valley.

"…another vision…" whispered Naz.

"No, Naz," replied Jerzuan. "No, I'm real! I swear! I survived. No, more than that. Naz, you have to get up. This is too important."

Naz clumsily pushed at Jerzuan and fell backward. "Begone Witch!" he screamed again.

He closed his eyes and waited for this vision to kill him. He hoped at least his death would be quick and painless.

"He will not believe you, Jerzuan," said a new voice. It was a woman's voice. One that sounded eerily similar to the disembodied voice from earlier.

"None of us really believed all this," replied Jerzuan. "We need to get him back to your hut, with the others."

"I agree," the woman responded.

Naz felt himself being lifted into the air. He was floating! Or at least it felt like it. It was all too much for him. Naz felt unconsciousness wash over him. Everything went black.

Chapter Seven

Drizzle still fell over Boron Nigh when Drew and Josh left their apartment. They approached Sergeant Walsh, the Protector that Balnather had appointed to watch him.

"We are leaving on Balnather's quest," Drew informed him.

Walsh nodded. "Very good," he said. "I shall inform the good Count."

"Good?" said Josh sarcastically once they were out of earshot of Walsh.

The duo followed the city streets toward the East Bay Protector Unit. Drew knew the eastern districts of Boron Nigh well at this point, having spent most of his time in this city there. As they wandered past the unit headquarters, Drew and Josh were stopped by one of the guards.

"Hey champs, we're we off too?" the guard asked.

"Balnather has sent us on a mission," replied Josh.

The guard laughed. "Yeah, what?" he asked. "Okay champs, gonna need youse to come with me."

Drew rolled his eyes. Firstly at his use of the term *champs* and secondly at the fact that this buffoon did not believe them.

Flatten him with the runes, said the voice in the back of his mind, but Drew ignored it, although this little runt would deserve it. Even his voice was annoying.

Josh looked at the guard with displeasure as he and Drew were shepherded to the unit headquarters. As much as Drew would not mind putting this chump in his place, he could not cause a scene. He just wanted to get out of Boron Nigh as quickly as possible. The guard led them into the building and approached a rather important looking Protector supervising the room.

"Hey sir," said the guard. "I found these two sneaking out claiming they're on a special mission."

The supervisor looked at him and then at Drew and Josh.

"Names?" he asked.

"Andrew Saran and Josh Gunnersbury," answered Drew.

"Ah yes, I got word from up above that you'd be passing through," replied the supervisor. "I apologise for this Cadet here. As you were."

The look on the guards' face was priceless as Drew jerked away from him.

"Good riddance," said Josh with glee.

Drew smirked as he passed the guard and they promptly left the building. Annoyed at the delay, Drew huffed and turned back toward the exit gates to the city. But as they approached the gates, Drew felt a hand on his shoulder. Turning around in frustration, he yelled out.

"What now!"

"Oh, er, sorry," said the familiar man before him.

It was Cron, one of Tenebrae's old bandit friends.

"Cron?" asked Josh. "What do you want?"

"Well, I, er. Saw you walk out of the Protector building just then and wondered what you two and Octavia were doing here in Boron Nigh?" Cron said.

"Wait... Octavia?" asked Josh. "Here? I thought he and Tenebrae returned to Dempair."

"Well, yes," replied Cron. "I saw him heading toward the dodgy part of town. Ya know. The West Bay."

"The entire place is dodgy, Cron," said Drew. "But I think I know what he might be doing. He's here to see Naz." He turned to Josh. "It's been a week since we came here, he's come back to meet with him."

"Naz?" echoed Cron. "Who's that?"

"A Protector up on Palace Rock," answered Josh.

"He's on our side, don't worry," Drew added quickly upon noticing that Cron had begun bristling.

"Pah!" he spat. "All those up in that place, they're all the same!"

Drew turned to Josh. "We should find Octavia," he said, ignoring the man's spiel. "Tell him we're about to set out... Ask him how Geetie has been the past week, and maybe if Tenebrae is already on her way to Hogs to meet us."

"And ask him to come with us?" asked Josh. "Of course, if Octavia could join us, it would be great. I mean, who cares what dumb rules Balnather has," he finished, referring to Balnather's insistence that Drew take just one companion.

"Ah, so you're not here together?" Cron asked.

"It seems it's a coincidence," said Drew. "Thanks, Cron. But now I think we really should go…"

"You! Peasant!"

The voice of the superior Protector from earlier rang in Drew's ears. He approached them, annoyance on his face.

"Mr Saran," he questioned. "Why are we talking to this lower born citizen?"

"Sorry, General Mortimus," replied Cron. "Mr Drew, I'll be off!"

With that, Cron bolted, Mortimus too slow to react, hence he turned back to Drew and Josh and did not bother to give chase.

"Well?" Mortimus asked. "Not giving away any secrets are we? I know one of the Great Leaders has entrusted you with a special quest." He leant in close. "You'd do well to keep that a secret from lower borns…" He turned to Josh. "*And* from your friends!" He stood up straight again. "Now go! Scram! Go on your mission and don't let me see you here again until it is complete!"

With that, General Mortimus turned and went back inside the unit headquarters. Drew stood motionless. He knew Octavia, his mentor and friend, would know exactly what to do in this situation.

"Let's go," said Josh. "But be alert – we both know that the West Bay can be rough."

But Drew was not listening, for inside his head, the voice had returned.

Those Protectors should have been obliterated by the runes, it said. *Do it! Go in and take vengeance on them! They dare not speak to us like that!*

"But we must find Octavia!" pleaded Drew. "At least we can tell him what Balnather's plan is." He gasped in shock. He was *talking* to this voice.

Josh looked at him in confusion. "Who are you talking to?" he asked.

Soon you'll learn to follow my instructions, Saran, said the voice.

Drew had no idea what had just happened. He knew that the voice was from his use of the runes, and that it had become more prevalent over the past few months, but it had never actually engaged in conversation before. He shook his head. He would find Octavia. Quickly, before any more Uprising Protectors could catch him, Drew ran off toward the West Bay, a confused Josh in his stead.

***

The west of Boron Nigh was even more down trodden than its eastern and southern counterparts. Here, buildings were in disrepair, a large percentage of street beggars were women and children, and some people lived out of tents set up on the side of the street. He gasped when he saw a family of six bundled up beneath a tattered old tarp just down a small alleyway. One question reached his mind at this sight. How had King Lakton allowed this? Were these substandard living conditions one of the reasons why the Uprising movement had been able to ascend?

Old me would have just blamed the Crownlands, thought Drew.

And though he knew a reopening of the main highway along the Greenarch Plain would certainly help, by the looks of his surroundings, the western part of Boron Nigh had been like this for a long, long time.

King Lakton ignores it, while the Uprising movement takes advantage of it, thought Drew sourly.

"Money sir?" asked one beggar, who had crawled up to Drew as he rounded a bend.

Drew took out a shilling and gave it to the man.

"Just one shilling?" he asked. "Please sir, do you have any more?"

Drew shook his head. "I don't, I'm sorry."

He had just thirty shilling cents remaining.

The beggar screamed in frustration. "Like the rest of them from the rich east!" he cried. "No money for the beggars!"

"My child is starving," started another beggar, accosting Josh. "Please, spare some money!"

Josh quickly spared ten shillings for her, before another beggar called out.

"And for me!" called the old woman, who was missing a leg.

The duo quickened their pace. Drew wanted to get out of this place.

Josh seemed anxious, and it appeared that unfriendly eyes were beginning to turn on the pair. Suddenly, a concerned voice piped up.

"Drew?"

Chapter Eight

Humans have always been fascinated with death – what happens when you die? For Naz, this question was now answered. Or so he thought. Death felt comfortable. It was dark, but comfortable. But so many fellow souls floated around him. Most of them were familiar. Jerzuan and Ketlaz, fellow Protectors in life, amongst others. He even heard Jemima's voice! He did not know how long he had been dead for, but since the Witch took his life he had decided that perhaps being dead was not so bad after all.

"Naz," whispered a voice softly.

Naz groaned. He wished it could just go away and leave him alone.

"Naz, try and open your eyes," said the voice again.

"Come on, soldier!" said the voice of Jerzuan.

Naz gave in and tried to open his eyes. To his shock, he realised that they indeed could open. He could see heaven for the first time!

"J-jemima?" he asked. "You're dead too? Jerzuan?"

Over him stood a woman. He had never seen her before, but she seemed young and pretty.

"Naz, you're okay," she said softly. "I am Horath."

"We're not dead," said Jemima. "Naz! The Witch... she didn't want to harm us." She paused. "Well, not exactly."

Naz shook his head. He looked at his hands. They were solid, no sign of blurring or any other traits that made it obvious one was in a dream. Here he was. Alive. And in a small, warm room. Naz sat up, feeling his strength returning. He was on his knees in Cold Valley one moment, and now he was safe.

"Have some green leaf," said Horath, passing him a mug. "Try and relax a bit. What you went through would have been quite a shock."

"You nearly killed him!" said Jerzuan, who had been sent to the valley in the patrol previous to Naz's.

"I have to keep our secret guarded, Jerzuan!" retorted Horath. "What if one of the commanders comes here in the next patrol, nay, the Chief Renault himself!"

"What is this place?" asked Naz. "Who are you?" he asked Horath.

"I am what you in Harleland refer to as the Witch of Cold Valley," she answered. "Once I practised witchcraft, many long years ago, before I was driven in this vale here after the practice was outlawed by Queen Lakila."

"But… it's said you are evil! And wicked!" Naz protested.

"A wicked witch, how original," answered Horath. "I kept to myself. Whenever intruders would come to my valley, I would use tricks of the fog to scare them away."

Naz looked upon Horath in confusion. This was the Witch? A fearsome entity, supposedly. She had tricked Octavia and

the others as they travelled to Hoonth, and she had attacked
Naz and his companions as they tried to capture her. Naz
realised with a jolt that she had purely acted in self-defence.
But another thing nagged at him. He looked at Jemima and
remembered his actions towards her before he was taken by
the Witch.

"Jemima," said Naz. "I-I'm sorry for how I spoke to you
earlier... I should not have told you to get out of my way."

"It's okay," answered Jemima. "At least I know what you
really think of me now." She seemed sad as she spoke the
last part of the sentence.

"Naz!" cried a happy voice. Trevault came into the room,
filling Naz's heart with joy.

"Trevault! You're okay too!" answered Naz.

"And all the others who Balnather sent here to Cold Valley,"
answered Trevault. "Big enough for an uprising!"

"The Uprising Uprising movement!" called Ketlaz, another
Protector sent to Cold Valley in a previous mission.

"No," answered Horath matter-of-factly.

"There must be at least ten Protectors here!" said Naz.

"Well, there's five of us in here – six if you count Horath,"
said Ketlaz. "Then there is Reke and Lilthyme outside too."

"Oh, trust me, I'm no Protector," said Horath.

"Oh, of course you are!" called Ketlaz. "You protected us down here! And I bet you'd make a formidable opponent to the Uprising Protectors back in Boron Nigh!"

Horath shook her head. "No," she said. "I do not wish to leave Cold Valley," said Horath. "It has been nearly a hundred years since I settled here. Here is where I shall remain."

Naz shuddered. A century of hiding away in this freezing place. It was unimaginable. Yet Horath still looked young. Like the past hundred years had not affected her at all.

"I can provide assistance from afar should you need it," Horath said. "But I do not wish to leave this valley."

Ketlaz nodded. "So be it," he said.

***

That evening, Naz felt well enough to wander out of Horath's hut. It was a simple little cottage, surrounded by a garden. Vegetables and herbs grew there, unimaginable considering the cold mist that swirled above. The sky was completely blocked by the mist, the grey cloud above the only sight one would ever see if they lived down here. Naz realised that there appeared to be some sort of bubble, a protective shield around the hut and the garden, preventing the fog from penetrating through.

"The fog is my protection from the outside world," Horath said, approaching from behind. "I did not wish to be hunted by rangers, but they were men who wanted to bring me back to Boron Nigh in exchange for a bounty. I had to hide away."

"I'm sorry that happened to you," said Naz. "The Crown doesn't hunt witches anymore. It's not exactly *legal* but it's also not something King Lakton cares about."

"It's for the best that I stay here," Horath said. "After all, the Uprising Protectors would not dare come here. This is a safe refuge for you all." She paused. "Say… do you know anyone by the name 'Saran?'"

Naz stopped. "Saran?" he asked.

"The others haven't heard of him," replied Horath. "Well, Reke said that he heard the name in Dempair, but wasn't sure."

Naz nodded. "Andrew Saran is a friend of mine," he said. "He's also a Protector. Reke is right – Drew is from Dempair."

"I can interpret signs," said Horath. "Witchcraft stuff, you know? The surface here in the valley has been restless lately and many rumours have come to my ears about someone named Saran."

"He passed through here once," said Naz. "Just a few months ago, on his way to Hoonth."

"Hoonth… Saran…" said Horath in amazement. "Yes! Saran was the Demi-god who had the gifts of shadows. It seems that his descendant is destined to save Harleland." She paused. "I do recall a group of Harlelish travellers coming through my valley not long ago," she admitted. "If Drew was indeed apart of that group, I will extend my deepest apologies for scaring him and his friends!" She laughed.

"I'm sure they'll all be glad to hear it!" laughed Naz in reply. "But Horath, how do you know about Drew's heritage and destiny?" he asked.

"Another Demi-god, by the name of Lazarka, a daughter of Harmales who was the second person to wed with a God," answered Horath. "She was given the gift of life. She speaks to me through the ground here sometimes." Horath paused. "She has told me that Saran's descendant must seek the root that breathes green veins."

"Cryptic," answered Naz.

Horath shrugged. "I don't get to decide what the gods' messages are," she answered. "But I do have an idea… There is an artefact. In Wilder Forest, guarded by their Duchess. Apparently a ley line runs beneath the entire forest, giving them a special connection to Lazarka."

"Nonsense!" said Naz. "Wilder Forest is a Dutchy of Harleland. If such a powerful artefact existed in our Kingdom, then we the Protectors would know about it."

"And the Crownlands didn't have any mysteries, did they?" retorted Horath. "Naz, back when I still lived in Harlelish society, Wilder Forest were always the most secretive Dutchy. They took advantage of low feudal obligations to the Crown and shared very little of what really happened there."

"The forests' Protector General, Sylvia, would never keep anything that significant a secret," said Naz.

"Perhaps she has… or she has not been let in on it," suggested Horath.

"Both are ludicrous," answered Naz.

Horath shook her head. "Naz, your task in this fight against the Uprising movement is to help these Protectors to rise up against them. From this place far away, we can only pray that Drew takes the right path." She smiled.

"I suppose you're right," Naz said. "But where do we even start? We need more troops if we're going to storm Boron Nigh and defeat the Uprising movement by force!"

"Well Naz, I think I have a friend who can help you in your mission," Horath responded.

"And what person would that be?" asked Naz.

"Well," answered Horath. "They're not a person. She's a dragon."

Chapter Nine

Octavia stood before Drew and Josh. The young Cadet gave a sigh of relief, while Drew removed his hand from the hilt of his sword. He noticed the old Protector handing out food to some rough sleepers.

"Octavia!" cried Drew happily. "I'm certainly glad to see you."

"And I, my boy!" replied Octavia. "What are you two doing in these parts? I thought you would have left already!"

"We had to deal with some annoying Cadet," replied Josh, referring to the guard that had obnoxiously hindered their progress earlier. Drew wanted to cast being called a 'champ' from his mind. "I've had better dealings with people from Palace Rock!" Josh finished.

At the mention of Palace Rock, Drew felt unfriendly eyes fall on him.

"He better not be one of Lakton's cronies," snarled a man as he ate the bread given to him by Octavia.

"That Balnather will sort the corrupt swamp out," said a woman next to him.

"We'd better get going," said Octavia. "Follow me."

With that, Drew, Josh and Octavia trudged along the street, getting closer and closer to Boron Nigh's western wall. The wall was badly damaged, either from poor maintenance, Herk attacks, or both.

"We truly are surrounded on all sides," said Drew.

"You understand now, why the Uprising movement has gained such traction," said Octavia, running his hand through his grey hair. "The wall just up ahead has a hole in it. It's how I get out of the city and sneak up to speak to Naz."

Drew nodded.

"Is it not guarded?" Josh asked.

"It used to be," answered Octavia. "Someone in authority somewhere at least knows about it. But not anymore." He paused. "Drew, how many Protectors did you pass on your way through the West Bay?"

Drew thought. "None," he answered. "Not a single one."

"Correct," said Octavia. "Lakton ordered all Protectors to be deployed to the east, south and to Palace Rock, when the Uprising movement first started to gain traction two years ago."

Josh looked at the old Protector in shock.

"So the past two years…" started Drew. "There have been no Protectors. No policing at all here in the western part of the city?"

"Not one," answered Octavia. "And Balnather has made it worse by completely cutting off Palace Rock save to those he personally summons." He looked around anxiously. "We've idled too long. Come, we must meet with Naz. Our weekly meeting is tonight."

Drew followed his mentor, Josh in their stead, as the trio reached the hole in the wall. A shady looking man sat at the exit and gazed upon them in glee.

"The toll to exit is ten shillings," he said.

"Ten!" said Octavia. "It was just five last week."

"I can make it fifteen if you want," replied the man darkly. "Now pay up."

Octavia reluctantly gave the man his money. But as Josh went to follow Octavia out of the hole, the man put out his arm and blocked his exit.

"Ten shillings *each*," the man said with glee.

Josh looked back at Octavia in alarm, and then turned to Drew. "I-I haven't got that much," he stammered.

"Oh dear, we are in trouble," said the man. "Looks like we aren't going anywhere." He clutched at a knife, ready to unsheath should Drew and Josh try and force their way out. Around them, two other shady characters also placed their hands on knives of their own.

Octavia seemed forlorn. He too had reached for his sword, hidden beneath his robes.

The runes, said the voice. *Use the runes, Drew! Obliterate these lower class peasants!*

Drew reached into his coat and withdrew his rune bag.

"Ah, so he does have the means to pay," said the man. "For the trouble, I've increased your toll to fifteen shillings!"

Drew smiled darkly.

"Of course," he said, as he took out a rune. "Pleasure doing business with you."

Octavia's eyes widened, Josh went to plead with Drew to stop, but they could not do anything as Drew yelled:

Kinetic.

A wave of kinetic energy exploded from Drew, knocking the three tollmen away and smashing the wall. It began to crumble as Drew raced out, a pile of rubble where the wall once stood. He turned to Josh, his apprentice joining him and Octavia outside the city.

"Quick, up the hill!" commanded Octavia. As they ran, he looked beside him at Drew. "What were you thinking, using the runes like that?"

"We had to get out of there," puffed Drew as he put his rune bag away. "I have the power of the runes, remember. I must use them!"

They halted a little farther up the hill.

Octavia rounded on him. "Andrew Saran, what did I say about being *careful* with those things!"

"You don't even know about the runes!" Drew cried back. "You had no idea what they were or where they came from. You have *no right* to lecture me on them!"

He felt his anger rising. He realised he was clutching at his coat, feeling the rune bag through the bearskin.

Octavia held a grave expression on his face. "We will continue this later," he said. He turned back up the hill, his eyes locking on to a tree farther up. "By the time we get there, Naz should have arrived," he finished.

Drew said nothing. Josh walked silently beside them, but his expression showed he had listened to the argument. Octavia had no idea what the runes could do. What they were doing for Drew.

I told you that you should have listened to me, said the voice. *Octavia is unwise.*

"I'm sorry," murmured Drew. "I will not ignore you again."

Octavia looked at him confused. Josh whispered something in the old Protector's ear, a look of grave concern coming across his face.

Good, answered the voice.

"Drew," said Octavia, turning back to him. "I need you. Harleland needs you." In a low and calm voice he added: "You cannot let those runes consume you. They *are* gifts. But they are gifts to be used wisely."

They walked on in silence, before finally coming to the tree. Drew gasped as he realised it hung over the wall. This was not any wall. On the other side of that was Palace Rock.

"Where is Naz?" wondered Octavia. As he went to climb the tree, Drew noticed something beneath the roots. Josh had noticed it too, and called out.

"What's that?" he asked.

"Hmm?" asked Octavia. But his eyes widened when he saw what Josh had pointed out. A locked notebook. "Oh no…" he muttered.

From his coat, Octavia produced a small key. He inserted it into the locked notebook and turned it. There was a click, and the lock released. Octavia opened the book and together, he, Drew and Josh read Naz's message.

"Sent to Cold Valley?" asked Drew in horror.

Octavia kicked a stone and yelled in frustration. "No! He was my only lead!"

"You can't talk to anybody else in the Protectors?" asked Josh. "You were the Chief!"

"All the others I was talking to were sent to that valley long ago," said Octavia. "And the ones that weren't stopped talking to me out of fear."

"What now?" asked Drew.

Octavia breathed. "The plan I had will need to be altered," he said. "We've lost our inside man."

"Come and find Prince Lekt with us," mumbled Drew. "Please."

"I can't, Drew," Octavia answered. "We need to proceed with great caution. Do not risk Balnather seeing you two travelling with me on the search for Lekt."

"Where could he have gone?" asked Josh. "Where do we start our search?"

"That was what I was hoping Naz would find out for us," Octavia answered glumly. "And now he's…" he broke off. "He's dead. Killed in Cold Valley."

Suddenly, shouts could be heard from down the hill. Protectors!

"Quickly, run!" called Octavia. "Make for Hogs! The Uprising movement doesn't have as much influence outside of Boron Nigh."

Drew nodded, and Josh signalled his understanding, and the pair ran off, while Octavia headed in the opposite direction. But to Drew's horror, his mentor ran into a unit of three Protectors who had come over the wall. He was detained, the three soldiers assisted by a unit of six who had raced up the hill from the damaged wall where Drew, Josh and Octavia had come from.

"Octavia!" called one of the Protectors. "Balnather will not be pleased by your sneaking around. Take him away!"

Drew's heart sank, while beside him, Josh breathed in fear. Now what?

Chapter Ten

The view was breathtaking, making Naz forget momentarily about his exhaustion. From this vantage point, almost halfway up the side of one of the Dirtgula Mountains, he could see the whole Greenarch Plain sweeping off toward the Crownlands. A river sat on the horizon, the River Harl, the border between the Central Dutchies of Harleland and the land that had declared the ongoing Civil War. As he looked to the east, he saw the marshlands of Dirtgula sprawling off towards the coast. A light brown line snaked its way across the marsh, the main road through Dirtgula between the Central Dutchies and the coast. The road was a feat of engineering, constructed over a century ago by Harleland in exchange for the then colony of Dirtgula joining the Kingdom. The road had to be built in a way where it would not sink into the soft, muddy earth that it was built upon. The road passed through Mudport's Mews, the capital of Dirtgula and Harleland's fourth largest city, before continuing onward to the Port of Dirtgula, far out of sight. Naz considered the scale of Harleland. It was a massive Kingdom, taking up the entire continent of Walgett. Yet Naz could see two entire Dutchies from up here. It was an incredibly clear day, not a cloud in the sky, and the beauty of the sight reminded Naz just why he and his friends were fighting so hard to regain their freedom from the several fronts that were trying to take it from them.

"I come up here sometimes to look at this view," the voice of Horath said.

Trevault and Jemima looked on in awe.

"It's beautiful," Jemima commented. She looked over at Naz and smiled.

Naz acknowledged her awkwardly and looked over at Horath.

"I thought you said you hated leaving Cold Valley," he said.

"I do," answered Horath. "I have no desire to leave this area."

She looked back down the slope of the mountain at the pit of fog that lay between this one and the next mountain along in the range. The broken bridge lay silent over the misty valley, a symbol of the fracturing of Harleland.

"When Lazarka spoke to me, weeks ago, she told me to come up here," said Horath. "Around here somewhere is an ancient cave system, the ancient tribes of the Harl Lands called them the Cursed Caves."

"And are they cursed?" asked Trevault.

"Everything around this place seems cursed," said Jemima dryly.

"The Cursed Caves used to be home to a Harl tribe called the Netherlings," explained Horath. "They practised witchcraft and wizardry there, however they were given their modern name by the later peoples of Harleland."

"They became the people of Lekt Valley, right?" asked Naz.

"That's right," replied Horath. "They founded Dempair, and the descendants of the Netherlings continue to live there to this day."

"So, the Dragon of Hoonth has settled in the caves?" asked Naz.

"She has," answered Horath. "To hide from Balnather and the Uprising movement. She told me that they wish to use both of us against the people of Harleland."

"Octavia and I were right then," said Naz. "Balnather, that *weasel*."

"His grotesque little nose puts me off everytime I see him," said Trevault in displeasure. "Naz, you met secretly with Octavia, right?"

Naz nodded. He knew now that Trevault and the others could be trusted. "Yes," he answered. "Once every week. He should have found my notebook by now." He lit up in excitement. "Which means he may be on his way here!"

"That's excellent!" cried Jemima. "He can lead us in our revolt!"

Horath said nothing, but a sadness seemed to show in her face. She shook herself.

"Come," said Horath. "The entrance to the caves is ahead. Kora is waiting for us."

"You know her name?" asked Naz as they walked.

Horath nodded. "She told me," she answered. "She seemed quite proud of it, actually."

Naz smiled. That information would please Drew. Where *was* Drew now? Did he know of the cryptic message that Lazarka had given to Horath?

Trevault spoke up beside Naz, breaking his thoughts. "Ever since I was a child I always hoped to see the supernatural," he said. "And now, I get to see the Witch *and* a dragon in just a few days!"

His excitement was palpable despite the grim circumstances of why they were here in the first place.

"Is that why you didn't follow Jemima and I back up the valley?" Naz asked, remembering with horror how an unconscious Trevault had been absorbed into the dark, fiery mist back in Cold Valley.

"I just wanted to see her," said Trevault. "And I did. But it was Horath. She looked like a young, fair woman, not this ugly witch that we'd been told lived there." He paused. "She told me to come with her."

Naz looked ahead at Horath. Her terror at being captured by the Uprising movement was clear. He understood why she put on such a fearsome show when they had originally wandered into the valley. It was a show that had, apparently, scared off Sergeant Elias, Kulu and Alfred. Horath said that she had watched them turn tail and flee. Naz thought it strange. That was out of character for Elias, who had usually been a brave and noble Protector. He shuddered. Perhaps they ought to look for him, and Kulu and Alfred as well, in case anything had happened to them.

"We're here," breathed Trevault in excitement.

Naz looked ahead. In front of them was a large entrance to a cave. Ancient markings were etched into the stone around the gaping hole. Naz looked at his companions. His eyes fell on Jemima, who noticed and stuttered awkwardly.

"You go first, Naz," she said. "I don't want to get in your way again." She seemed shy and unsure of herself.

"Jemima," began Naz exasperated.

"Leave it," said Trevault, giving Naz an annoyed stare. "Let's just get inside."

Naz guiltily allowed himself to be herded by Trevault into the cavern. Horath and Jemima followed. The temperature seemed to drop instantly once inside. Naz gasped. The ceiling was glowing a brilliant blue. It seemed almost that millions of stars glowed above.

"This is incredible!" said Trevault in amazement.

"What magic is this?" asked Jemima.

"Glow worms," answered Horath amused. "Perhaps it is magic. Or perhaps it's just natural."

"Glow worms!" said Trevault in excitement. "I never thought worms could do magic!"

Naz was pleased that his friend was happy. Even if it was just because of some glowing worms.

"Horath," said a new voice, stopping Naz in his tracks.

"Kora," called Horath in response. "It is good to see you again."

In the gloom, two purple eyes appeared, floating in the dark. Naz took a step back in fear, Jemima behind him doing the same. Horath stood her ground like this was expected, and Trevault actually took a step forward.

"Oh Dragon, is it really you?" he asked.

"Trevault of the Protectors," said the voice, the distorted voice of an elderly female. "Your willingness to learn of the unknown, your excitement… it is a vital component for peace."

Drew never mentioned the dragon could talk, thought Naz.

"Drew never needed to talk with me," said Kora, reading Naz's mind, and coming forward now into view, her black scales reflecting in the brilliant light of the glow worms. "It was not the right time," she finished.

"H-how…" Naz stammered.

"I can ascertain the thoughts of those around me if I deem it important to know them," Kora answered. "Equally, I can converse with the Demi-gods to obtain the knowledge necessary to convey to you. And you, Naz, are the most important one here."

Naz looked at the dragon in shock. "Me?" he asked. "Why?"

"If it were not for you, Octavia would never have known to send someone to come here for you."

"Who?" asked Naz.

Kora ignored him and continued. "If it were not for you, then Horath would not have been briefed on Drew's quest and of his membership of the Saran family. And if it were not for you, then there would be nobody to lead the final battle against the Uprising movement."

"Me, lead that?" asked Naz, stunned. "But surely Octavia will do that when he arrives? He'll have found the notebook by now! Right?"

Kora shook her mighty head. "It seems, from what I can see… Octavia found the notebook. But he is… captured. The rest is too hazy and I cannot see."

"*Captured!*" called Naz in shock. "No! He can't be!"

"Maybe he can send for someone?" asked Trevault. "Maybe Sergeant Elias will find us and lead us again."

"Your leader is already among you!" said Kora with clarity. "Naz. This is your quest, as finding Prince Lekt is Drew's quest. *Both* of you must succeed in your separate tasks to ensure the destruction of the Uprising movement. Only then can the Civil War with the Crownlands be ended."

Kora withdrew back into the darkness and closed her eyes. She was gone.

"Wait!" called Naz. "I need more guidance." He turned to Horath in desperation. "Where do I start?"

"You are the Protector here, not me," answered Horath.

"Naz, this is your chance!" said Trevault. "Remember when we were both cadets together? We went to Cernsland for a camp. We fought off a bunch of thugs who tried to rob a bank. *You* came up with a strategy on how to defeat them."

Jemima nodded. "You've already been leading the internal resistance to defeat Balnather and his cronies," she said.

"That was Octavia," answered Naz. "I was just helping him."

"He wasn't on the inside though," said Trevault. "You were. Right in the middle of it all up on Palace Rock. You risked *everything* helping Octavia considering where you were. I was there. I would not have dared do what you did."

A grunt came from deeper in the cave.

"Kora probably doesn't want us hanging around yelling in here," said Horath in response. "Let's go back to the valley."

Naz nodded in agreement. One by one, the four companions left the Cursed Caves and began the descent down to Cold Valley.

Chapter Eleven

Drew huffed as dawn broke. It had been a long night as he and Josh raced down the slopes of Mount Merthru. The land beneath them had levelled out sometime ago, and he realised they must have entered the Dutchy of Hogshire at some point. Drew stopped to catch his breath, Josh coming in beside him. His head still spun after the events of last night. Octavia had been captured, putting the quest to stop the Uprising movement and the Civil War on the edge of a knife. Before him, lights glittered in the early morning shadows. Hogs, the capital of Hogshire. It was here they were to meet Tenebrae, in two days from now. He thought once more about his task, given to him by Balnather, yet endorsed by Octavia for different reasons. Prince Lekt was missing, whether he had genuinely disappeared or had been sent away by King Lakton on some secret mission was still unclear. And Naz! The revelation that their inside man had been sent to die in Cold Valley still hung heavy over their heads.

It's all gone wrong, thought Drew miserably.

Their pace had slowed as the sun rose. Josh looked tired, the young cadet struggling to keep moving.

"We're nearly at Hogs," started Drew. "We can rest there while we wait for Tenebrae."

"I could sleep for days," said Josh, a yawn stifling his speech. "I haven't been this tired in Lakton knows how long."

"Imagine," continued Drew. "A nice hot breakfast, a bed to sleep in… We only slept in beds yesterday!"

"It feels like an age since we left the apartment in Boron Nigh," said Josh. "Say, does Balnather live there sometimes himself?"

"He says he rents it, like an investment or something," replied Drew.

"Ah great," said Josh. "So Balnather's a landlord too!"

"Does your father rent out houses to people?" asked Drew.

Josh shook his head. "He only ever focussed on his food stalls," he replied. "I wonder how he's doing, back at the orphanage."

They walked in silence for a while, the sun rising higher in the sky.

"What's the first place we should look for Lekt in?" asked Josh after a while.

Drew shrugged. "I can't imagine he'd have left Harleland, so he must be somewhere in the Kingdom."

"It's a big Kingdom," said Josh.

"It seems like we'll have to search all the Dutchies and Counties if we're gonna find Lekt," said Drew.

He shuddered. That would mean they would have to go to the Crownlands. He thought of what would happen if he were to come face to face with someone like his uncle, Count Michael. Or even the Lord of the Crownlands himself, Duke Shârvous.

After another hour of walking, Drew and Josh finally arrived into the town. Hogs was similar in size to Dempair, if a little larger and certainly much more welcoming. Unlike his home village, Hogs seemed to have a bustling main street. It was a stark difference to even Boron Nigh. It was almost like the Civil War with the Crownlands and the take over of the Uprising movement had no effect. Drew smiled as he walked along the main street. The duo decided to rest a while in the first tavern they found, aptly named the *Wild Hog Inn*. They entered the pub, Drew hoping this time not to be accosted for money by some drunk like at *The Sparkling Miracle* back in Boron Nigh. The inn seemed pleasant, it was a light and airy room and it put Drew's worries at ease.

"Welcome," said the barmaid, waiting for him at the counter. "A drink today, sir?"

"Just a place to rest our heads," Drew replied. Suddenly he remembered his lack of money. He gulped. "Oh, ah… how much first?"

The barmaid shrugged. "How long are you staying for?" she asked.

"How long does thirty shilling cents let me stay for?" Drew asked.

"Make it forty, I have ten shilling cents…" said Josh, his exhaustion showing.

She laughed. "Ten minutes. Unless you want to clean the dishes on top of that?"

Josh looked forlorn.

Drew shrugged. "Well, if that works."

The barmaid led Drew and the reluctant Josh behind the bar and showed them their work. Josh groaned when he saw the pile of plates, bowls and utensils piled up.

"Our kitchen hand walked out last night when he saw that," the barmaid said. "You're really saving my neck by cleaning this for me."

"I just want to sleep," complained Josh, and though Drew agreed with his apprentice, he was thankful for being able to stay at all despite their lack of money.

Damn that beer I had the other night, he thought.

For the rest of the morning, Drew and Josh scrubbed away at the utensils. They were both bone tired. Exhausted. Drew barely remembered being dismissed and shown the room he and Josh would share. When he finally lay down, he was out in an instant.

***

Drew stood on a wooden platform high above the trees. Wait. Was he still Drew? An intrusive thought pierced his mind. The voice of the woman he was now inside the head of.

"Queen Wilder," said a voice. A guard approached, looking at her forlornly. "Elder Len wishes to see you now."

*"It is time then," Queen Wilder responded. She felt
apprehensive. According to the customs of Wilder
Forest, the queen must listen to her elder. The elder was
like a Royal Advisor, someone who would give advice to
the King or Queen, such as in neighbouring Harleland.
She prepared to go, to do her duty. As she walked, she
reflected on the reports her spies had given to her from
beyond Wilder Forests' borders. Discontent was rife in
Harleland, and King Merthru had fallen out of favour
with the Emperor. Harleland, a client Kingdom of the
Augustan Empire, was so far away from the rest of the
empire. It meant that there was a growing desire from
the Harlelish to declare independence. Yet there was
also a feeling of pressure for Wilder Forest. Several
Protector units had come to Wilder Forest and their
other neighbours the Crownlands, itself a sovereign
Grand Dutchy. They had asked for Wilder Forest to join
them in a new Empire as a show of strength against the
Augustans, however Queen Wilder had no desire to
declare vassalage to Merthru. This sacred Queendom
had existed for thousands of years, its people deep in
sync with the Demi-god of Life, Lazarka. Her gifts gave
the people of Wilder Forest hope and power. She did not
wish to give that all up just so Harleland could appear
strong enough to their Emperor in order to gain
independence. However that was what her meeting today
with Elder Len was all about. Harleland had already
vassalised the colony of Dirtgula, on the east coast of
Walgett, and Cernsland to the north had also joined
King Merthru. It was now just Wilder Forest and the
Crownlands. Arriving at the meeting point with Elder
Len, the Queen looked over her Queendom, observing
the Sisters of Lazarka as they conducted their nightly*

ritual. She sighed. Wilder remembered when she was still a member of the sisterhood, before Elder Len had chosen her as the next Queen. How she had tended to the Springs of Yore, a thermal spring whereby the Warriors healed, the ones charged with the defence of the forest. She was distracted by a noise, and she turned to see Elder Len making his way towards her.

"My Queen," he said, bowing.

"My Elder," Queen Wilder responded, bowing also.

"It is time," Elder Len continued. "We must decide. Harleland has begun placing sanctions on our Queendom."

"We cannot give in to these bullies," said Wilder. "Wilder Forest is a sacred place, and we are its protectors. Who knows what could happen if people from the outside gained control over us."

Suddenly, the world went silent. A booming voice, dripping with power, rang out to all present.

The root will breathe green veins.

"My Lady!" cried Elder Len.

Wilder looked out in shock. It was Lazarka's voice. The Demi-god of Life had spoken.

Suddenly there was a flash of green. Into Queen Wilder's hands there fell a seed. Len looked at her in shock.

"The legend of the Green Tree," he said. "That seed is the foetus of Lazarka. She must be planted!"

Quickly, Wilder raced down from the great tree where her ancestors had built the Queen's palace. She ran over to the Sisters of Lazarka, who had looked up in awe when their Demi-god had spoken.

"Sisters!" called Queen Wilder. "Please. Pray for this seed. Pray for Lazarka to be reborn as the Green Tree, to bless the land of Wilder Forest for millennium to come."

Suddenly, there was a cry. Smashing through the forest, fearsome battle-ready soldiers were pouring into the clearing.

"No!" called Wilder. "You will not take my forest by force!"

As she surged forward, Drew was left behind, a bodiless soul floating invisibly in the air.

Chapter Twelve

Horath looked up sharply.

"Someone draws near," she said. "I can feel someone entering my valley."

Naz gasped as he saw Horath float off the ground. They had all been strategising how best to invade Boron Nigh and overthrow the Uprising movement when Horath had felt an intruder. Horath rose her arms and the mist above them began to swirl and turn dark. Balls of fire were shot from her hands. Seeing this power from the source intrigued Naz. He watched enchanted as the Witch of Cold Valley lit up the black swirling fog. She flew upward and out of sight, the fiery mist crackling like a thunderstorm. Yet here beneath it all they were safe.

"More of us, you think?" asked Jerzuan.

"I can't see who else," said Naz. "I guess Horath can't be too careful."

"It's incredible," commented Trevault. "To see the Witch at her full power, in person." He gazed up in wonder.

"I wonder who else would get sent here?" asked Jerzuan.

"I saw Illfracombe questioning one of the Sergeants just before we got sent here," replied Lilthyme.

Naz sat in silence. He hoped of course for it to be Octavia. But he knew after what Kora had said that it would not be. He had been captured. Possibly even being tried for treason back in Boron Nigh as they spoke. He hoped what the dragon had predicted had come to fruition, perhaps. Maybe Octavia could have sent for someone, and they were now here.

"Whoever is up there is probably terrified right now," laughed Jerzuan.

"I also like to laugh at other people's misery," said Reke dryly.

"Oh, piss off Reke," said Jerzuan. "We don't want the joke police around here."

Reke shrugged. "At least make the humour good," he said.

"Humour is subjective," replied Jerzuan.

"Oh shut it, both of you," said Lilthyme with a smirk. "Anyway, how long does it usually take for Horath to bring the newcomers down?"

"It took ages to get Naz, Trevault and Jemima down," said Reke.

"Take as long as you want," said Trevault, transfixed.

So the group sat there for the next several minutes, the howling storm of fire and mist sounding above. Naz twiddled his thumbs.

***

It was over after a few more minutes. Three exhausted shapes could be seen. A fourth shape, Horath, landed before them all.

"You'll die, you monster!" called a familiar voice.

Sergeant Elias! Naz realised.

The three figures emerged from the lightening mist. Indeed, Elias was there. Beside him was Kulu! And the third. It was Geetie Gunnersbury!

"Sir!" called Trevault. "And Kulu!"

"What is this devilry?" asked Elias. "It can't be! Trevault!"

His eyes widened even more when he saw the others. By now, the rest of the Protectors had come out of Horath's cottage and stood in her garden before the new arrivals.

"Jemima!" called Kulu, as the two friends ran over and embraced.

"Naz!" called Geetie. "Wait, that *is* you, right?" He approached Naz cautiously.

"It is," he responded. "What are you doing here? You were in Dempair running the orphanage, according to Octavia."

"Octavia sent me!" cried Geetie. "Or at least that's what that scruffy old guy said… Cron, I think he said his name was."

"Kora was right… He *did* send someone after us!" called Naz in excitement. "Is it true?" he asked. "That Octavia has been captured?"

"Well, yes, but…" said Geetie "Wait, how did you know? Cron delivered Octavia's message to me just a few days ago… I assumed you would have been down here longer than that."

"I found your dragon," explained Naz. "Long story."

"Kora?" exclaimed Geetie. "Ah, she is okay then! And please, do tell me your tale! I love stories. I even took the liberty of packing in my harmonica should we want some music! I regret to say my Lyre was too big to pack in on this particular journey."

Naz smiled. "You are exactly the way Octavia described you when he told me the tale of the quest to the Great Tower," he said.

"Anyways," continued Geetie. "I ran into these two on my way down from Lekt Valley. The orphanage master looked around at Sergeant Elias and Kulu. "They were looking for you, I was looking for you, so we travelled together. And here we are!"

"What happened to Alfred?" asked Naz, as Sergeant Elias approached them.

"That coward?" spat Elias. "He ran back to Boron Nigh with his tail between his legs. No doubt Count Balnather and Chief Renault will know you where all taken by the Witch. Well, let's just hope he didn't know you survived…"

"We're starting a revolution, sir," said Naz. "I'm not sure if you are for or against the new regime, but regardless of what you say, all of us here plan to march on Boron Nigh."

Elias nodded. "My boy," he said. "It would be my absolute privilege to join you." He turned to the others. "Damn Balnather!"

Cheers went up from all present.

"Would you like to rest?" asked Horath. "I'm sorry, but I have to appear like I did to ensure that all those who enter my valley do not cause me ill."

Geetie shook his head. "No," he said. "I want to know everything that's going on here.

"I agree," stated Elias. "Naz, you sound like the leader of this operation… Where do we start?"

***

Naz looked around at the eager faces of his comrades, feeling the weight of their expectations. He took a deep breath, trying to gather his thoughts. They had all crammed into Horath's cottage, all eleven of them. Naz, Trevault, Jemima, Kulu, Elias, Reke, Ketlaz, Jerzuan, Lilthyme and Geetie, the nine Protectors, the food merchant-turned-orphanage master and Horath, the Witch of Cold Valley. Sergeant Elias spread an old and worn map of Harleland out on the table before them.

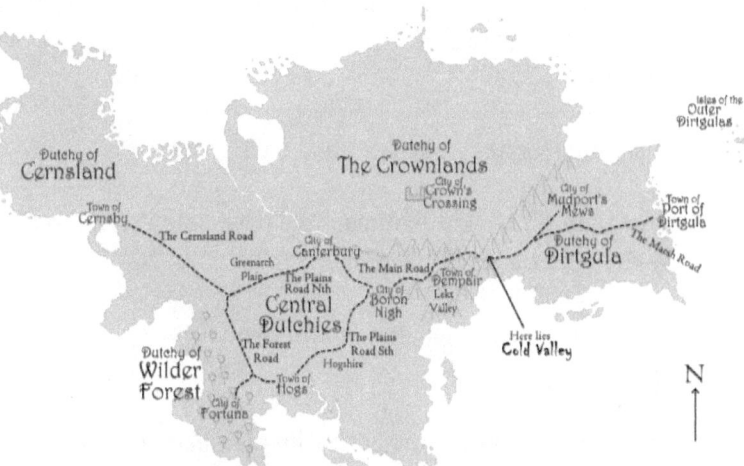

"It's a long march back to Boron Nigh, with the main road blocked by the Herks," he started. "And we're a big group."

"The Crownlands will see us for sure," said Reke. "How do we avoid them?"

Naz shook his head. "The fact that we're such a large group will mean that the Herk patrols won't dare to challenge us."

"They'll send for a battalion though!" cried Jerzuan.

"But we're not hanging around," retorted Naz. "Look – if we take the main road along the Greenarch Plain, it will take a day to Boron Nigh. If we take the route we took to get here, along the base of the mountains, it will take several days."

"But that's on horseback," said Kulu. "It would be two days on foot."

"I have some horses here," said Horath sadly. "I do not wish to part with them, but… if it's for the greater good, then you may have them."

"Thank you, Horath," said Trevault.

"I agree with Naz," said Jemima. "We have nine Protectors. Most Herk patrols are formed of just four or five."

"We'll have nearly double the troops," said Ketlaz thoughtfully.

"And by the time they come back with their battalion, we'll be long gone," finished Naz.

"Naz, my boy," said Elias. "I have only one question."

Naz stared at him.

"Why in Lakton's name did they make me a sergeant and not you?"

Chapter Thirteen

Drew awoke sweating. He sat bolt upright in his bed. The vividness of the vision made the experience he had just had feel all the more terrifying. He looked around the dark room. Josh slept soundly in the bed across from him. He did not want to wake his cadet, but he had to say something. Without thinking, Drew started talking.

"I just had a dream," he said aloud to himself. He knew no one was listening and that Josh was fast asleep, but he had to talk. He had to. "I-I saw everything from Queen Wilder's point of view."

Queen Wilder? he thought.

He knew that *Duchess* Wilder controlled Wilder Forest, and that it had been almost two centuries since Wilder Forest had last been an independent Queendom. Nowadays it was a Dutchy of Harleland, although similarly to Dirtgula and the Crownlands, was not part of the Kingdom's Central Dutchies.

"It must all connect," he said to the darkness again. "Prince Lekt disappearing, this vision…"

The last time Drew had a vision like this was when he was in Wiln. He had seen King Zinton talking with one of his advisors as they discussed the threat of the now defeated Voksenkollen Tribe. That had been an important vision. *This* surely must be an important vision too.

And I'd held the runes that night, remembered Drew.

He looked down at his body. Sure enough, the rune bag was snuggled safely in his arms. Perhaps the voice could explain it.

"How does it work?" he asked it. "The visions. Do I have them whenever I sleep with the runes in my arms?"

There was no response. Perhaps the voice only spoke when it suited *it*. Drew gave up waiting for a response and got out of bed. He opened the window and looked out. It was late he realised. It was not yet midnight, but in another hour the day would turn. He was unsure if Tenebrae would arrive earlier than the three days they had agreed upon. The only reason they were here now was due to the fact they had run most of the way after what had transpired in Boron Nigh. He paced the room, his anxiety slowly easing as he listened to the quietness of the night. At last, Drew returned to his bed and tried to sleep. It came eventually, but only after laying awake for several hours.

***

A rooster crowed from a nearby farm. Drew awoke, tired still after spending most of last night awake in his bed. He looked over at Josh. He did not want to wake the cadet, yet the sooner he could discuss his vision with Josh, the better.

He shook himself and decided upon a morning stroll. Hogs was supposedly a pretty little town and seeing it in the nice morning sunshine seemed like a nice idea. The accommodation, *The Wild Hog Inn*, was very homely, and despite his angst about the situation he and Josh were in, Drew did certainly enjoy the simple task of dishwashing he and his friend had performed earlier. Maybe he could become an innkeeper when all this ended. It seemed a simple life.

Drew went around the block, stepping out into the cool morning air and marvelling at the neat streets and nice trees and gardens. This small town was slightly bigger than Dempair, yet it was so much nicer than his home. He did not think it was possible for such a nice town to exist in Harleland in its current state. After a steady walk of about an hour, Drew returned to the inn and made his back up to the room. He noticed Josh still sleeping. His apprentice had overslept.

"Josh," Drew whispered, gently shaking his apprentice.

"Hmm?" murmured Josh. "Oh, it's you?"

"We must look for Tenebrae," said Drew. "The sooner we find her, the sooner we can all get out of here and start properly looking for Prince Lekt."

"Tomorrow is the third day," yawned Josh. "You think she'll be here early?"

"If I know Tenebrae, she will be," said Drew. He sighed. He realised now was a good opportunity to tell Josh about his vision. "Josh, last night… I had a dream. A vision, like I did back in Wiln."

Josh sat up. "The runes again?" he asked. "They let you have those visions, right?"

Drew nodded. "Yes," he admitted. "I saw Wilder Forest! From the past. And then there was an attack! I think it was

Harleland…" Shame washed over him. Had his Kingdom taken over Wilder Forest by force all those years ago?

"Drew," said Josh. "Remember what Octavia said. Not all is well in Wilder Forest! And now this vision!"

That was when it all made sense. A memory came to Drew. Ker Gorûn had told him! His grandfather had told him all the way back in Hoonth!

Find the root that breathes green veins, he had said. That was also what Lazarka had said in his vision!

"We must go to Wilder Forest!" said Drew with excitement.

"Agreed," said Josh. "All the signs are pointing to it. And I'd be willing to bet that's where Lekt is, too."

They made their way out of the room, Josh closing the door gently behind them and making their way downstairs. The bar staff were preparing for the day's service.

"Oh, on your way out now?" piped up the exhausted looking barmaid from earlier. She must have been up working until early in the morning, only to be starting again for the new day just hours later.

"For now," replied Drew. "We're looking for one of our friends who will meet us here. Her name is Tenebrae. If she comes here, can you tell us?"

"Of course!" replied the barmaid. "You will be back tonight?"

Drew shrugged. "That all depends on if she shows up today or not," he replied.

"Well, those dishes in there will be waiting for you if you do!" said the barmaid.

"Oh great," muttered Josh.

With that, Drew and Josh left the pub and walked back out into the sunny mid-morning. Drew had spotted the western exit of Hogs on his walk earlier and looking at one of the maps of Hogshire, realised it led straight to Wilder Forest.

"I think we ought to scout that road," said Drew. "I'm still not sure how safe it is to travel the highways at night. It'll probably be crawling with Herks."

"You think it'll be safer to travel off road?" asked Josh.

Drew nodded. "I think so. "From what I can ascertain the land is quite flat, and there's very few trees between here and Wilder Forest." He paused. "We shall have to travel without light so we can't be spotted from the road."

The duo walked on toward the western exit of Hogs. With the day moving on, Drew became even more worried that they would indeed need to spend another night at the inn. Josh seemed to share his fears. His apprentice stared longingly out at the road.

"The sooner we're on our way, the better," he said. "And look! I think I can see the tree line of Wilder Forest, right on the horizon!"

Indeed, a faint blue line seemed to stand out on the edge of Drew's vision. It was more than likely the first trees of Wilder Forest.

"I wonder if Prince Lekt truly is in there," he wondered.

***

Night had fallen when Drew and Josh returned to the inn. After a day of wandering the town of Hogs, there was still no sign of Tenebrae. It seemed they faced another night here waiting for their friend. However as they entered the inn, the barmaid called them over in a hurry.

"That Tenebrae girl you told me about," she began. "She was here before!"

"Really?" asked Drew in excitement. "Where did she go?"

The barmaid shrugged. "She said she was heading out to look for you. She mentioned something about the western highway towards Wilder Forest."

Josh turned to Drew. "That doesn't sound right," he whispered. "Surely she would have stayed here and waited."

Drew nodded in agreement. "I think it's worth following up though," he said. "And if she's already at the western exit, then it means we can head off straight away."

They turned back to the barmaid.

"Thankyou!" Drew called.

"My pleasure," the barmaid replied.

Making their way out of the inn, Drew and Josh made their way through the dark streets of Hogs, finally coming to the edge of town and looking upon the road that led into the inky darkness of rural Hogshire. Josh gulped, and Drew looked forward anxiously. He had camped alone in the dark before, when he travelled for the first time from Dempair to Boron Nigh, but…

… *then I got accosted by Brig and those Herks,* he thought with fear.

No. The moment Tenebrae found them; they would have to push on. They needed to get to Wilder Forest as soon as they could. Octavia was counting on them, nay, the entire Kingdom. Drew took a step forward to scout a little way ahead. His confidence was enough to inspire his cadet to follow him, Josh stepping into the darkness and following his mentor onward. They did not get to walk far though. A figure appeared before them, and soon three more surrounded the duo. Drew gasped with horror. He recognised the armour these four men wore. Crownland armour. They were Herks.

"Come with us," the leader said. "Bind their mouths so they can't alert the Protectors!"

His charges obeyed, and Drew and Josh were led off the road and into the darkness of the undergrowth that lay a little way off.

"Can you see, Tyront?" asked the leader.

"Barely, Captain Crysthan," answered Tyront. "The moon is covered."

Drew's arms were bound. Josh struggled next to him, but two of the Herks held the cadet's arms tightly. They walked for over half an hour, navigating the gloomy hills and dips of Hogshire, until finally the light of a fire came into focus.

"The camp!" called Tyront.

"Finally," said Captain Crysthan. "Those sad sacks of dung had better have found food for us too. I'm starving."

They came into the camp. Two more Herks awaited them by the fire.

"Captain!" they both called, saluting.

"At ease, Herks," answered Crysthan.

"This is the one that our Caller told us about?" asked Tyront.

Caller? thought Drew in shock. Someone had ratted them out to the Crownlands!

"Yes," replied Crysthan. "Unbind this one's mouth." He motioned to Drew. "His little apprentice here needs not speak." He smirked at Josh, who scowled back at him.

One of the Herks who had held Drew roughly pulled down the cover that had gagged his mouth.

"Speak!" demanded Captain Crysthan. "Why are you on the road to Wilder Forest?"

"Just… a regular patrol," said Drew. "Just let us go, we aren't harming you!"

"Not until we find out why a Protector and his apprentice are wandering alone through the night," growled Tyront.

"And so far from home," added Crysthan. "She did say you were strangers to Hogs."

"Maybe he doesn't want his new masters finding out about his mission, milords!" squealed one of the other Herks in excitement.

"Ha!" laughed Crysthan. "This Uprising movement has made our job even easier. Why do you think we've drawn back on raiding the villages of Harleland?" He sneered at Drew. "Because why waste Crownland lives when we just need to sit and wait for your petty Kingdom to destroy itself."

"Shut up, scum!" cried Drew, but he realised with fear and loathing that they were right. Despite the Greenarch Plain now being controlled by the estranged Dutchy, smaller raids, particularly on Dempair, had become almost non-existent. Yes, their Caller Brig was dead, but there had not been a raid on Dempair for over two months. Perhaps the Crownlands *were* just biding their time for the two factions of Boron Nigh to destroy themselves.

"I'll ask you again," said Crysthan, heating his sword in the fire.

Drew's eyes widened as the Herk Captain approached, his red hot sword placed near to Drew's arm. He could feel the heat radiating from it.

"Why are you going to Wilder Forest?"

"T-to convey with Duchess Wilder!" cried Drew. It was true that he would probably speak with her. But he could not give away that Prince Lekt could also be there.

"What are you conveying with her?" asked Captain Crysthan. "And was this an order from the Uprising movement or from Petty King Lakton?"

Drew spat at him. Crysthan looked at him in anger. He took his red hot blade and swung it towards Josh. The cadet cried in terror through his mouth gag as the blade stopped just before his face.

"What," growled the Herk captain. "Are you *conveying* with her! Tell me! Or this *kid* gets it!"

"An order from… The Uprising movement. It was a secret mission from Inquisitor Balnather himself!"

"Inquisitor who?" asked Crysthan.

"Someone named Balnather milord," answered one of the Herks.

"Sounds like the name of a dick," said Tyront.

Drew wanted to say he agreed with them, but he pushed the feeling away and focused on the situation at hand.

"What is your name, weasel?" asked Crysthan.

"D-drew," answered Drew. "Drew… Gunnersbury." He looked over at Josh who nodded in understanding. Drew knew better than to use the name 'Saran.'

"Drew Gunnersbury," answered Crysthan. "Not related to that Geetie Gunnersbury, are you?" he smiled cruelly. "Captain Dirk gave us all a mighty gift when he burnt that manor down. It was *full* of riches."

Drew looked over at Josh and signalled to him to keep it together, but it was clear that he was livid at the Herks. Josh screamed something through his mouth gag, a strong swear word Drew imagined. Josh's trauma was evident and justified. Drew relived the moment again, when Geetie and Josh's manor had been burnt to the ground after a Herk named Grimster dropped a flaming torch as he and Captain Dirk escaped. Drew remembered the shock, horror and hatred of the Herks plastered on the face of Josh as he and Geetie were forced from their home. Regrettably, with the Crownlands conquering of the Greenarch Plain, the manor still sat ruined, unable to be rebuilt until the filthy Herks had been driven away.

"Captain," started Tyront. "Should we kill them?"

Josh looked at his mentor in terror. Drew stared up at the cruel captain with bated breath.

Chapter Fourteen

Five horses sat at the ready, what little gear the Protectors still had with them bound to their sides. Naz sighed. These poor beasts were pets, not war steeds. He had double and even triple checked with Horath that she was sure she was happy to lend them her horses. She assured them all that it was fine.

"Simple maths," Naz had ordered. "Two of us per horse. Geetie, you're with me. I want a briefing on what's been happening in Dempair and beyond. Trevault and Jemima. Let's see, Reke and Ketlaz," he continued. "Elias and… Kulu! And that leaves Jerzuan and Lilthyme."

The Protectors plus Geetie each organised themselves into their pairs and climbed aboard their horses. The peaceful beasts grunted under the weight of supplies and soldiers. Naz again looked at Horath.

"It's okay, Naz," she said. "Just… if you can, bring them home. When all this is over."

"I can't promise they'll all survive," muttered Naz. "I can't even promise we'll all survive. But if they do, you have my word."

Horath nodded. "Then good luck, all of you," she said.

"Onwards!" called Elias.

They rode upwards, Horath lifting the fog to allow them to see their way forward. Naz looked ahead. Geetie sat behind him, a sword hanging from the side of their brown splotched steed. He was not sure if Geetie was combat trained, however the merchant's decision to bring the blade with him from Dempair clearly showed his willingness to fight if needed. They rode in silence until they reached the top of the valley. Naz breathed and closed his eyes. He was out. After so long, he was free of Cold Valley.

"Tell me everything you know, Geetie," he started.

"Well, the orphanage is untouched," started Geetie. "Marlo seems angsty though. Tenebrae and I suspect that Balnather is growing impatient with his inability to capture the Witch."

"Has he made any policy changes?" Naz asked.

"Well, not that I've seen," Geetie replied. "Although the cadets were all made to go to a special camp at Bunglemere Heights, which is strange because they only just got back from one last month."

"And what of Tenebrae?" asked Naz.

"After Cron delivered Octavia's message, she decided to look for Drew and Josh," explained Geetie. "I decided to come here... Well, initially I wanted to find my son. But we needed to find you, and you know." He sighed. "Josh is a big boy now. He doesn't need me protecting him anymore." Geetie almost choked that last part out loud.

"He is making a fine Protector," said Naz. "You should be proud of your son. I have no doubt he and Drew will find Prince Lekt." He paused. "I wonder why the cadets got sent back to another camp then?"

Geetie shrugged. "I think it's because the Uprising movement is concerned that the cadets in the orphanage are too loyal to Octavia. Poor young Hermit wanted to come with me to find you, but he was sent away to the camp by Marlo."

"Hmm," wondered Naz. "The sooner we get back to Boron Nigh, the better."

They rode onward, the empty highway of the Greenarch Plain taking them closer to the capital. They had not encountered a Herk patrol yet, but Naz knew it was inevitable.

The horses trotted steadily, their hooves clopping rhythmically against the hardened earth. The Protectors rode in a disciplined formation, their eyes scanning the horizon for any sign of trouble. Naz's mind was a whirlwind of thoughts and plans, trying to anticipate the challenges they would face on their journey. Suddenly, Trevault cried out. Naz looked beyond his friend and saw the shapes of four Herks.

"Swords at the ready!" called Elias, brandishing his blade.

The four Herks seemed to talk quickly amongst themselves before fleeing.

"Ha!" laughed Jerzuan. "Those filth have run away!"

"Run away to call a battalion!" said Elias. "We need to pick up the pace."

"I agree," ordered Naz. "Let's go."

But they had barely gone forward another five minutes when a Herk patrol blocked their path, ten angry Crownland soldiers bristling with rage.

Naz and Elias rode forward with purpose. "You are blocking Royal Protectors from using the road," called Naz. "Move aside!"

The lead Herk wandered forward to meet them. "This road belongs to the Crownlands," he called. "It is the property of Lord Shârvous."

"Lord now?" asked Naz. "Last I heard he was still a vassal of King Lakton."

He smiled in a taunting way at the Herks. This made them angrier.

"Get off our road, you filth!" cried the Herk captain. "Or we'll throw your corpses off it."

He unsheathed his sword. His fellow Herks began to approach, blades in hand also.

Naz nodded to his Protectors. He and Geetie dismounted their horse, and their other eight companions brandished their blades. An arrow from Kulu began the battle, ten Herks against nine Protectors, Geetie falling back with Sergeant Elias. Naz became locked in combat with the lead Herk, smashing his sword into his, a parry breaking out between them as swords and clubs smashed around them, the clang of steel ringing through the air. Naz and the Herk captain's swords continued to meet in a flurry of blows, each seeking to gain the upper hand.

Another of Kulu's arrows found its mark in the throat of one Herk, dropping him instantly. She quickly notched another arrow, scanning the melee for her next target. Trevault and Jemima fought back-to-back with skillful coordinated strikes cutting through the enemy ranks with precision. Reke and Ketlaz used their agility to outmanoeuvre the Herks, darting in and out to deliver quick, lethal blows. Elias barked a warning for Jerzuan, as the sergeant blocked an incoming attack with his shield, before kicking his Herk assailant in the throat. The Protectors fought like a well oiled machine, years of training on display. There was a reason these nine had been selected to serve at Palace Rock.

"You traitors have torn our Kingdom apart!" yelled Naz to his foe. "But no longer."

"All Lord Shârvous wanted was a *fair* arrangement with the Crown!" the Herk captain yelled back, as he bore down upon Naz once more with his sword.

Naz blocked the blow and twisted around, swinging his blade at the captain, only to also be skillfully blocked. Yet around them, it had become clear that the Herks had lost the battle. Two Crownland soldiers lay dead, and the others were being slowly driven back.

Noticing this, the Herk captain spat at Naz and broke away.

"You may have won this skirmish," he cried. "But Lord Shârvous *will* have vengeance on you all." He started backing away. "Herks! Retreat!"

The surviving Herks joined their captain and ran off, the cries of victory from the Protectors singing out behind them.

"We can't idle here," called Naz over the celebrations. "We must move on. Boron Nigh is another several hours away."

"Agreed," said Elias. "Let us go."

With that, they climbed their horses once more and rode onward.

Chapter Fifteen

Captain Crysthan thought for a moment. Drew knelt before him, waiting to hear his fate.

"Don't kill him yet," Crysthan decided. "There's still more information I want to get out of him. But first." He paused and looked around. "I'm starving. Is dinner ready yet, you two morons?"

Crysthan turned to the two Herks who had stayed behind at the camp.

"Well we found some rats, sir," one started. He pulled a roasted rodent off from the fire where it had been cooked on a spit roast. "Tasty!" he said.

Captain Crysthan looked upon the meagre meal in disappointment. "You swine," he said. "Resorting to eating rodents. But you couldn't even catch a deer in sunlight!"

"Sorry sir," burped the other, his stick from the meal laying on the ground beside him.

"They'll call us savages!" complained Crysthan. "Fine! Give me one, but do not say a word of this to Count Michael."

Count Michael! thought Drew in anger. His uncle, the wretch who had ordered the assassination of his father and the one who had hoarded all his grandfather's wealth for himself.

"You two mites," called Crysthan. "Stand guard over Gunnersbury and his cadet."

"Yes sir!" called the goons.

The two Herks who had dragged Drew and Josh all the way here handed them over to their half-witted companions and joined Captain Crysthan and Tyront for dinner. Josh sat beside Drew now, the cadet's mouth still gagged.

"I'm Murk!" started one.

"And I'm Irk!" said the other.

"And I didn't ask," said Drew glumly.

"Aw, cheer up old mate!" said Murk. "You just need to accept that we Herks are better than you!"

"It must hurt, being spoken to like that by Captain Crysthan," said Drew, an idea forming in his head.

"Well, I guess," answered Irk. "But it's for our own good! That's what Count Michael says anyway."

"Well, he sounds like a bully to me," said Drew. "And you know what? Fearsome Herks of the Crownlands like yourselves should stand up to bullies like him."

Murk shrugged. "It's just the way it is," he said.

"We get rewarded greatly you know," said Irk. He smiled darkly. "Murk and I got shares from Gunnersbury Manor." He looked down at Drew with contempt. "Sorry about that."

Josh bristled next to him, but he could not speak with his mouth still bound.

"What, is he your uncle or something?" asked Murk.
"Geetie."

"Oh, yes," answered Drew. He had to change tact.
"Truthfully… we don't get along. In fact – no. I'll wait until
your captain has finished his… meal."

"Aw, you can tell us!" said Irk with excitement.

Josh looked at Drew questioningly.

"Well I can tell you want to prove yourselves to Captain
Crysthan," said Drew. "How about a deal."

"As long as it doesn't involve us letting you go," growled
Murk.

"Get me one of those cooked rats – I'm starving," said Drew.
"Then I'll tell you. And you can say to Crysthan that *you* got
the information out of me."

"So be it!" said Irk in glee. "I'll go over and get one now."

The Herk soldier let go of Drew and walked over to the fire.
He grabbed a rat on a stick and came back over.

"I can't eat it with my hands tied!" said Drew.

Murk rolled his eyes. Reluctantly, he cut Drew's bonds.
Drew grabbed the stick and began to eat. The rat was stringy
and tough. He had eaten earlier at the inn, so he was
certainly not hungry enough to want to eat the rat. He just
needed to pick the right moment.

"It's good," he lied.

"Well, thank you," said Irk. "Maybe you Harlelish people aren't as bad as we thought."

"I went to Boron Nigh when I was a kid," said Murk. "It was a little family holiday, you know?"

"Before the war," sighed Irk. "I lived near the River Harl. I used to love walking along its banks, before it turned into a battlefield."

Drew could not believe he was feeling sorry for the Herks. But as much as he sympathised with them, the knowledge that these two wretches had looted Geetie and Josh's home, the conduct of Captain Dirk, the wretched Count Michael, as well as his need to escape to Wilder Forest, made him act. Irk was staring out at the dark fields surrounding the camp, and Murk's hold on Drew's right arm had loosened. Quickly, Drew pulled away from Murk and smacked his arm away with the stick. He reached for his sword and unsheathed his weapon, brandishing it as the Herks all turned toward him in shock. He swiftly cut Josh's bonds, and the cadet unbounded his mouth. The Crownland soldiers in turn unsheathed their blades and looked upon the duo in contempt.

"You fools!" screeched Crysthan.

Irk lunged forward at Drew, the pair becoming locked in a parry, while Murk went after Josh. Drew kicked Irk's leg and smashed his head with the hilt of his sword. The Herk screamed in pain as Drew raced backward, standing clear of the attackers. Josh had managed to fight off Murk, and came in beside his mentor. They were outnumbered, and would surely lose if they tried to fight all of them.

"Need help?"

It was the voice of Tenebrae. She had finally come! She came in beside Drew and Josh, as the four Herks came closer, more wearily this time with an extra foe to face.

"So, there are *three* of you now," growled Crysthan. "The plot thickens."

Tyront started the push from the Herks, and Drew and Tenebrae fought back to back, sword and knife in hand, while Josh primed his bow and arrow. A good strike from the apprentice saw Tyront's arm impaled, and he collapsed unconscious from the pain.

Drew knew there was only one way to end this quickly. He withdrew the runes.

"Tell Duke Shârvous to go jump!" he called as he held one of the stones in his hand.

Beam.

One after the other, each Herk was knocked backwards by his shadowy beam of power. The trio turned and fled, Drew knowing the Herks would be unable to pursue them any further. As they ran back toward the road, Drew noticed dawn beginning to break overhead. He and Josh had spent far too long sidetracked with escaping from Herks. After almost forty-five minutes, they finally arrived back at the road, the main highway between Hogs and the entrance to Wilder Forest finally underneath their feet again.

"Dratted Herks," said Josh miserably.

"You took your time," said Drew, looking angrily at Tenebrae.

She stared back at him defiantly. "You said three days, and tomorrow is the third," she said dryly. "It's lucky I heard that commotion as I was sneaking into town just before."

"Yeah, well–" started Drew, but Josh stopped him.

"It's okay Drew," he said. "We're all together again now, the quest can continue. And she *did* save our lives."

"Very well," muttered Drew. He was unsure why he was so upset at Tenebrae, yet he guessed it was probably something to do with the runes.

They trudged slowly along the road, the sun climbing higher. Off in the distance, the dark green treetops of a forest could be seen. Their destination! It still seemed a way off, much to Drew's disappointment. The road wound on, twisting this way and that, the green fields and sparse forests of Hogshire surrounding Drew, Josh, Tenebrae and their lonely road on all sides. He wondered who the Crownland Caller was. His guess was the barmaid, since she would have had all day to sneak off to tell the Herks, made even more obvious by her saying Tenebrae was waiting exactly where the Herks were. He gasped as he realised that he and Josh had been sent right into a trap.

***

It was mid-morning. The sun had well and truly risen, and despite the winter chill earlier, Drew had started to feel hot. The heat did not seem to bother Josh and Tenebrae all too much however, his apprentice walking confidently beside him as they gained on Wilder Forest. Tenebrae was walking along cheerfully, as if she had forgotten their argument the night before. Drew's constant looking over his shoulder to see if Crysthan and his cronies had followed them had ceased a while ago. That was because he could see the eaves of Wider Forest before them. The trio walked the final few metres toward a large silver gate. It was closed, yet no fence seemed to exist around it. Drew knew better than to just walk around however, as before him were two guards, dressed in green gowns and wielding spears.

"What brings you to Wilder Forest?" one asked.

"I am seeking…" started Drew, catching his breath. "I have been sent here on a special mission. We are looking for Prince Lekt."

The guards stood silent. Suddenly, the gate opened.

"You are permitted entry," they said. "The Prince awaits."

Chapter Sixteen

The Protectors stood before the gates of Boron Nigh. Naz drew breath in anticipation. This was it. In order for this siege to work, Naz knew that they had to rely on the other Protectors within the city's walls joining them in turning on their new Uprising masters.

"Well," said Elias, beside him. "It all comes down to this, doesn't it."

"I haven't felt like this since we arrived at Hoonth," said Geetie as he disembarked from his horse. The five peaceful beasts were battered but they would survive. Naz was glad. He hoped for them to pass peacefully back to the Cold Valley where Horath undoubtedly awaited them. The Herks should have no business harming innocent horses, well, he hoped so anyway. He cast his mind back to what Drew had told him once. Naz's very own horse, that Drew and Tenebrae had escaped from Boron Nigh upon, was burned in the carnage of Geetie and Josh's manor after Crownland soldiers invaded. Drew and Tenebrae had been apologetic about the ordeal, and Naz had rightfully been upset that his steed had been stolen and led to their death. But his steed was clearly a Protector's horse, and certainly a target of the Herks. He hoped that these five would be seen by any Herk patrols as what they were – pets.

"Safe passage, horsies," said Trevault, giving the horse he and Jemima had shared one last pat.

The horses whinnied and then began trotting steadily back the way the company had came. The Protectors looked at

Boron Nigh. The gate was silent. Yet they knew they were being watched. Naz stepped forward and cleared his throat.

"We are here to liberate the people of Boron Nigh!" he called. "We call on all Protectors that are still loyal to the people to join us in overthrowing the Uprising movement!"

Silence.

"This is anti-climatic," muttered Elias.

Suddenly, several arrows were shot towards them.

"At arms!" ordered Elias, as the nine Protectors withdrew their weapons.

"You are committing an act of treason!" called a voice from above the gate.

Naz recognised the voice as that of General Beftoh Kern.

"Stand down Kern!" called Elias. "You know the Uprising movement has torn the Kingdom apart!"

"I serve whoever holds command of the Protectors!" Beftoh called back.

"Then you're a fool!" screamed Elias. He turned to Jerzuan, Reke and Ketlaz. "You three, start climbing that wall. We'll cover you!"

The three nominated wall climbers nodded in their obedience and ran over to the wall, pressing themselves against it to avoid a fresh flurry of arrows. Naz gasped as hot coals sitting in a bucket atop the wall were thrown down by the guards.

Lilthyme called out to the three in warning, and they dived out of the way. The hot coals exploded onto the ground and a small grass fire broke out on the lawn.

Jemima withdrew her bow and notched an arrow. She shot it, piercing a guard atop the wall. They dropped dead.

"Jemima!" blurted Trevault. "You killed a fellow Protector!"

"It's war, Trevault," retorted Jemima. "Until we can free Boron Nigh from the Uprising movement, there will be many more deaths. You can be sure of that."

By now, the fire had begun to surround the main gate. The blaze had grown even more fierce, and Naz knew there was no way through. Jerzuan, Reke and Ketlaz were all stuck on the other side. Naz caught Reke's eye and nodded. Reke nodded in return and he went back to climbing the wall with his two companions.

"We can't leave them in there on their own!" called Jemima.

"We must make for the hole in the wall by the West Bay," said Naz. "That's where Octavia used to sneak out to meet me."

Elias nodded. "Let's not waste time then!" he ordered. "Lead us on Naz."

"Follow me!" Naz called as he began running, the others in his stead.

By now, he had no doubt that messengers would have reached Balnather and the Inquisitors. He wondered what twisted words Renault would have for the Protectors within the city. On they ran, aware of arrows still being shot from the wall. Finally, after several minutes, the clean, well kept lawn ended and the companions began trekking through the rugged landscape that sat outside the western wall of Boron Nigh. Then he saw it. A broken piece of the wall! Naz gazed at it confused. He was sure that Octavia had told him there was a hole in the wall, but the sight before him now was that of a pile of rubble. He gasped. Four Protectors stood guard by the collapsed wall, while workers went about trying to rebuild it.

"Stop them!" came a cry from the guards as they continued to chase them on top of the wall.

The four guards unsheathed their swords nervously.

"S-sergeant Elias?" one asked.

"Jordan!" Elias cried in joy. "I'm glad to see someone I recognise!"

Suddenly there was a cry of pain. An arrow from one of the guards atop the wall had found their mark. There was a gasp of shock as Naz whipped around. Trevault stood there with an arrow through his neck.

"Well," he puffed. "I hope I served Harleland well…"

He dropped dead. Geetie gave a cry of agony, while Kulu and Jemima angrily fired a flurry of arrows back, missing their shots as they became overwhelmed with fury and sadness. The four Protectors before them appeared torn with who their allegiance should lie with. Naz did not care. He stormed into the city of Boron Nigh, Elias in his stead.

"Join us!" screamed Elias. "Protector or not, join us and take back our Kingdom!"

The peasants around them all gave cries of cheer. The four wall guards cheered also, joining the Revolt of Boron Nigh. Five Protectors had become nine again, along with Geetie and an army of the fed up people of the West Bay of Boron Nigh. And Naz was their leader, walking confidently in front of the army. Their pursuers from earlier could only watch in awe as the battalion marched onwards. Soon, they spilled out of the western part of the city and onto the main street of the capital, leading from the main gate to the stairs up to Palace Rock. Some Protectors joined them, others tried to fight them, the only certainty being chaos. Naz, Commander of the Revolt, led them all on. Soon they passed the East Bay Protector Unit, who themselves put up a fight. Naz found himself locked in combat with General Mortimus, the pair trading blow after blow, while around them, people continued to march forward, windows were smashed, houses were looted and all around the rules and laws of the city were thrown out the front gate of Boron Nigh. Eventually, Mortimus was bested after Jemima jumped in to help Naz to finish off the fight.

"Join us, General!" called Naz. "This is it. We can destroy the Uprising movement!"

Mortimus sneered. "Never!" he cried.

Naz looked down on his defeated foe in disappointment. "So be it," he declared.

With that, Naz and Jemima joined the rest of the army as they arrived at the locked doors to the staircase that led to Palace Rock. They banged upon the doors, but Naz knew they were enforced with steel.

"We need a ram!" cried Naz over the noise.

Elias nodded. "In the armoury!" he cried. "Boron Nigh keeps a battering ram in the main armoury, not far from here!"

"I'll take some Protectors and fetch it!" Naz said.

He saw Kulu firing arrows up at the top of the gate, trying to pick off the guards as they poured buckets of hot coals upon the army. They could deal without him for a while. Naz turned and to his delight saw Jerzuan, Reke and Ketlaz. They had successfully climbed the wall! A small army of peasants accompanied them. Naz and Geetie both recognised Cron amongst them.

"You mad men are actually doing it!" Cron cried in delight.

"We have to get that gate down first!" said Geetie. "Naz, I'm not much of a fighter! I'll join you in going to the armoury to fetch the battering ram."

"We need at least ten to lift that thing," said Naz.

"We'll all go together," said Jerzuan. He scanned the crowd, the noise of the battle ringing loud in their ears. "Where is Trevault?"

Naz hung his head. "He didn't make it," he said sadly.

Jerzuan's face hardened. His expression turned sour.

"Let's get that ram," he said. "And then ram it up Balnather's ass!"

With that, Naz, Geetie, Jerzuan, Reke, Ketlaz, Cron and the other peasants marched to the armoury.

Chapter Seventeen

Drew felt a mix of relief and trepidation as he, Josh and Tenebrae stepped through the silver gate into Wilder Forest. The air here was different, cooler and filled with the scent of pine and moss. Ancient trees towered above, their thick canopies casting deep shadows that made it feel like twilight despite the morning sun. The path ahead was narrow, winding through dense undergrowth that seemed to swallow any sound, creating an eerie silence.

As they walked deeper into the forest, Drew could not help but feel a sense of awe. The forest was alive with a magic he had never encountered before. The leaves seemed to whisper secrets, and the ground beneath his feet pulsed with energy. He knew he was entering a place of ancient power, a sanctuary for those who sought refuge from the turmoil of the outside world.

On and on the path went, the trio not meeting a single person despite walking on for what seemed like hours. Drew was aware however of life all around him, and he heard the sounds of creatures in the undergrowth. Birds sang in the trees around him, and he saw glimpses of squirrels, possums and all manner of small animals going about their business. He closed his eyes and breathed. This place was heaven on earth. The serenity, this wonderful forest, free from the troubles of the outside world, where war and death reigned.

Soon, they came to another gate. It was silver, like the gate at the entrance to the forest, and on the other side was a bird bath. A large, green and red parrot washed themselves in the water, the most beautiful bird Drew had ever seen. The parrot gazed at Drew with its large dark eyes and then took off majestically, flying high into the canopy above and out of sight.

"Mr Saran," called a voice.

Drew whipped his head toward the sound in surprise. From the undergrowth beside the bird bath, a woman emerged, dressed similarly to the guards outside the forest.

"I am sorry if I startled you," she said. "I am General Sylvia, the head of the Warriors of Wilder Forest."

Drew noticed long blonde hair extruding from the silver helmet upon her head. She held a wooden spear, small green leaves growing from its sides.

"I expected someone to come find us," said Drew. "The guards said that Prince Lekt is waiting for me?"

"Indeed," replied Sylvia. "And your friends, Josh and Tenebrae."

Josh looked at Drew mischievously. "I thought Drew was the important one," he said with a smirk.

"You are three of the five," explained Sylvia. "The five who journeyed to the Great Tower. Your importance cannot ever be understated."

Josh's face became plastered with the biggest grin Drew had ever seen. Tenebrae beside him was also in high spirits from Sylvia's praise. He was happy for his apprentice. No more than a boy when he first set out from his manor on the

Greenarch Plain, Josh Gunnersbury was now a Protector through and through.

"Follow," said Sylvia.

Drew, Josh and Tenebrae obeyed, following her along the now wider pathway beyond the bird bath. Drew gasped as the trees became older, larger and closer together. Strange lights hung down from the canopy above, and he realised that they were now entering a city. Beautiful wooden houses lined the road now, and people were going about their everyday life. In the centre of the city was an ancient tree, a large and grand door at its base, and brilliant lights hanging from its branches high above. Beside them was a large square of grass, a group of seven nuns, it looked like, practising a ritual.

"This is the city of Fortuna," explained Sylvia. "Named so after the fortune that was blessed upon the inhabitants of Wilder Forest by the gods."

"We're finally here!" exclaimed Josh.

"Now we just need to speak to Prince Lekt," said Tenebrae, looking at Drew in concern.

General Sylvia nodded. "He is with Duchess Wilder now, within the palace," she said.

She motioned toward a great, ancient tree that towered above them all.

"Thank you," said Drew. He paused. "Octavia said not all is well here."

Sylvia nodded. "Not all is well everywhere in Harleland," she explained. "But that will be for my Lady to explain to you. For now I must return to the frontlines." She nodded a gesture of farewell. "It seems, Mr Saran, Mr Gunnersbury, Ms Tenebrae, that the fate of Wilder Forest may be in the hands of you and the growing rebellion back in Boron Nigh."

Drew nodded. "We will do what we can."

With that, Sylvia departed. The trio turned back toward the ancient tree.

"The Palace of Wilder," said Josh. "Apparently, the ancient Queens lived there, and it remained the home of the Duchesses after Wilder Forest joined Harleland."

"This… is still Harleland," Drew breathed in amazement. "But how? Why? This place feels different. Like it should be its own realm."

Tenebrae looked ahead darkly as they walked. "Perhaps it should be," she said.

"From what my father taught me," began Josh. "Wilder Forest supposedly joined Harleland freely. Back in the Independence Wars, when Harleland broke away from the Augustan Empire."

Freely? thought Drew. *My vision implied that they were conquered by force!*

Finally, they arrived at the entrance. Drew took a deep breath as he entered the tree palace. He was amazed at how similar

the Palace of Wilder felt to the Great Tower. The spiral
staircase went up through the trunk of the tree, and a great
pale green light glowed from above. In the middle of the
trunk, small glowing insects buzzed about their business,
their glow bouncing off the brown bark of the tree. Soon,
voices could be heard. Drew gasped as he recognised the
voice of Prince Lekt. Finally, the staircase ended. In front of
them, a great platform extruded from the side of the tree,
overlooking the grassy square where the nuns were
conducting their ritual. Two figures stood upon the platform,
Prince Lekt was one, and the other was the most beautiful
woman Drew had ever laid eyes on. She had curly blonde
hair, a great green dress, and a tiara made of ancient wood
upon her head, small green leaves growing from it, similarly
to the spears that the soldiers had all held. They both turned,
Lekt looking at Drew in relief.

"Andrew Saran!" he called as Drew and Josh approached.

The Prince held out his hand and Drew shook it.

"I am glad to see you here!" he said again.

Drew was nonchalant about meeting Lekt again after last
time. He remembered the council meeting at Boron Nigh,
after he and his friends had returned from the Great Tower.
Lekt had agreed with his father that they should ignore Ker
Gorûn's message to treat with Duke Shârvous.

"So," began Drew. "I believe you have some explaining to
do about your disappearance."

Lekt looked solemn. "My father sent me here," he said. "Come, sit with me. I am sure you three are exhausted from your journey."

Drew was much obliged, and Josh and Tenebrae both sighed in relief when they sat upon the wooden chairs that sat upon the balcony. Soon, servants dressed in similar style to the Duchess came and delivered them food and drink. Some remained behind after delivering the goods to play a gentle music. Now sitting with a plate of food before him, Drew turned to Prince Lekt.

"Wilder Forest has something," the Prince began. "An ancient artefact that we could use to turn the tide of the war!" He paused. "I 'disappeared' so that the Uprising movement was not alerted to our plan."

"What about us?" asked Josh. "Does your father still not trust us after we bought him Ker Gorûn's message? Couldn't you at least tell Octavia where you were going?"

"My father is distrustful of everyone these days," admitted Lekt. "He is still upset about Gorûn's message. That is why he sent me here, to use the power of this supposed artefact."

Beside them, the woman observed silently. She noticed Drew looking at her in wonder. She smiled.

"I am Duchess Wilder," she explained. "It is good to meet you, Andrew Saran."

"And what do you think about all this?" asked Josh.

"I think that King Lakton needs to keep his hands off Wilder Forest's ancient protector," she said.

Lekt scowled. "But as I have said many times now, Duchess Wilder! The very existence of Harleland depends on this!"

"And I say to you Prince Lekt, as *I* have said many times now – my response is the same as Ker Gorûn's. Stop the fighting."

Lekt hung his head. "But Wilder Forest's existence is threatened too," he pleaded. "The Herks have begun pushing into the northern eaves of your land, felling trees for firewood!"

"All the more reason for you and your father to hurry up and meet with Duke Shârvous," said Wilder. "Agree to a truce. End this Civil War."

"But you said it yourself!" began Lekt again. Wilder looked upon the young Prince with annoyance. "The reason you skipped that council meeting weeks ago, the day Drew came back from Hoonth! You had to stay here and help defend your Dutchy from the Crownlands."

"I know what I did," said Wilder calmy. More firmly, she added: "And I am telling you once more, Prince Lekt. The answer is *no*."

Drew looked at her. What must she truly think of all this? Watching the Kingdom that her ancestors had pledged vassalage to, either by choice or by force so long ago, being torn apart.

"My Lord," Drew asked. "What can Wilder Forest do to help Boron Nigh destroy the Uprising movement that another Dutchy like, say, Dirtgula can't do?"

Prince Lekt looked at Drew in silence, and then motioned toward Wilder.

"In the days before Wilder Forest joined with Harleland," Wilder began. "The Demi-god of Life, Lazarka, gave our Queendom a great gift," she explained. "It was a seed, the foetus of Lazarka herself, that when planted would sprout a tree–"

"The Green Tree…" Drew said suddenly.

Wilder looked at him in shock. "How did you know that?" she asked.

"I had a vision," he declared. "I saw it. The day that Harleland invaded this place." He looked at Prince Lekt accusingly. "And took it by force!"

Josh gasped. Lekt looked at Drew in horror. But Duchess Wilder shook her head calmly.

"No, Drew," she said softly. "Your vision was wrong. It was not Harleland that invaded Wilder Forest. It was the Crownlands."

Chapter Eighteen

Naz led the way, his heart heavy as he again thought over the loss of Trevault. He was full of determination, steadfast in his goal to ensure his friend had not died in vain. The sounds of battle echoed through the narrow streets of Boron Nigh, where the clashing of steel and the cries of combatants mingled with the scent of smoke from fires that had broken out. The city of Boron Nigh was in ruins, order replaced with chaos, and Naz had to suppress a feeling of anxiety over the fact that he had caused this.

No, he thought to himself. *Balnather and the Uprising movement caused this.*

Beside him, Geetie, Jerzuan, Reke, Ketlaz and Cron marched forward with purpose. An Uprising Protector lunged at them, Reke and Jerzuan engaging in a duel with their new foe.

"Go!" yelled Reke. "We'll hold them off!"

Naz nodded, and the remaining companions set off. Once more, they were accosted by Uprising Protectors, those soldiers who had remained loyal to the Inquisitors brandishing their blades in challenge. Naz and Ketlaz fought side by side as they parried with their respective foes, Geetie standing back in fear. The merchant held his sword before him, but the gravity of the situation had clearly borne down upon him.

"Cron!" yelled Naz. "You must get Geetie somewhere safe!"

"No!" called Geetie. "I'm with you to the end! Cron, take me to the armoury! We must get that ram!"

"Eye!" said Cron in response. "C'mon Geets."

Naz whipped around and blocked another blow from an Uprising Protector. He screamed in horror as a blade plunged through Ketlaz's chest. His ally's lifeless and bloody body dropped to the ground, and his foes began creeping closer. Naz gave a cry and ran after Geetie and Cron. There was nothing more to be done here. He pelted down the narrow streets of his city, the sounds of terrified civilians coming from all sides of the road. On and on he ran, emotions coursing through him, as he looked for the armoury. Ketlaz was dead, and so soon after Trevault's passing. This was indeed a bloody and brutal revolt.

The armoury had a large brick tower extruding high in the air, a place where guards could watch over the city from the very centre of Boron Nigh. Naz had finally caught a glimpse of it, and to his surprise, the top of the tower was deserted. Perhaps the Protectors who had been stationed up there had come down to join the fray.

"Naz!" called Geetie. He was in the armoury, poking his head out from behind the doors.

Naz rushed over to the unguarded entrance, Geetie ushering him into the building and slamming the doors shut behind them. The chaos outside sounding now as just a deep echo on the other side of the thick stone walls of the armoury. Cron, as well as several peasants from the streets of Boron Nigh, were busy rifling through the various weapons and arms.

"Here!" called Cron, beckoning for Naz and Geetie to follow.

There it was, Boron Nigh's battering ram. A massive, iron-tipped battering ram mounted on a wooden frame with wheels.

"Quickly, get it ready!" Naz ordered.

Suddenly, he felt a knife at his throat. He heard Cron groan in annoyance, and an unpleasant voice hit his ears.

"Well, well, well," it said. "What have we here? Naz the Protector! A valiant effort indeed."

Naz realised the voice spoke from the loft above them. His attacker was one of the peasants that had accompanied Cron, and he was able to turn his head and look at the former bandit. He too was being held by one of the peasants, while Geetie was nowhere to be seen.

"Turn him towards me," ordered the voice.

Naz was turned toward the voice, and he looked up in displeasure to see Count Mossjoint, the Uprising Inquisitor.

"Lie to me and die," the miserable Count said. "We know from our *prisoner* that you and Octavia met in secret!"

Naz said nothing. He looked up at Mossjoint in hatred.

"How did you escape the Witch? Where is Andrew Saran!" His eyes narrowed. "And where is Prince Lekt."

"You sent Drew to look for Lekt *yourselves* you buffoon!" cried Naz.

"And after all this time, he is still not back!" snarled Mossjoint. "But no matter. King Lakton's health has... deteriorated. Lekt will have to come back before his father's death, lest we take the throne for ourselves!"

"You lie!" spat Naz. "Lakton is getting old, but he still has many long years left!"

"That is where you are wrong, Naz," Mossjoint replied. He seemed serious. "King Lakton shall pass, and the three Inquisitors of the Uprising movement, myself, Count Hoop and Count Balnather shall reign supreme as the Great Leaders of Harleland."

"Fool!" Naz screamed in anger. "You don't think Balnather would conquer you both in an instant? He's the real leader of your stupid movement!"

"You underestimate me," said Mossjoint. He smiled. "Since you're about to die anyway, as a matter of fact, I agree that there should be one leader of Harleland, and that leader shall be *me*–" He said no more and instead gave a startled cry.

Count Mossjoint collapsed dead, the blade of Geetie Gunnersbury running through the Uprising Inquisitor's chest. Geetie stood over Mossjoint victorious. The peasants looked around confused, before fleeing. Naz and Cron stood together in the empty room, with Geetie looking down upon them from the loft. The merchant looked forlorn.

"I've... never killed someone before," he stammered.

Naz shook his head. "You have to keep going Geetie," he said. "We have to wheel this battering ram back to the gates of Palace Rock."

"Is it true?" asked Cron. "About Lakton?"

"I don't know," replied Naz, as he moved in behind the ram. "He was starting to look quite frail these past weeks, I must admit. And Mossjoint seemed serious."

Geetie descended from the loft and moved in beside Naz and Cron. He looked pale, clearly still coming to terms with taking a life. The trio pushed with all their might against the battering ram. It moved, but it was slow, and Naz knew this method was unsustainable. Just at that moment, two guards burst in, looking at Naz in recognition. Despite this, they still stood with swords drawn and pointed at the trio and their battering ram, although they showed some hesitation.

"Stand down!" Naz commanded, though he realised he was tiring. He was running only on adrenaline at this point. "We need the battering ram. This is our only chance to take back Boron Nigh."

The guards exchanged glances. "We were ordered to defend the armoury," one of them said, though his voice wavered.

"Do you want to defend the Uprising movement?" Geetie asked. "Or do you want to stand with your fellow Protectors and the people of Boron Nigh?"

The hesitation was palpable. Finally, the guards lowered their weapons and stepped aside. "We're with you," the first guard said.

Naz nodded in gratitude. "Please," he said. "Help us push this thing."

They nodded. "F-for King Lakton…" one murmured.

The other looked at his comrade as if he had not heard those words in an age.

"For King Lakton!" he yelled, more sure than his companion.

So it was that Naz, Geetie, Cron and the two guards pushed the battering ram out of the armoury and back through the streets of Boron Nigh. From around them, fellow Protectors and civilians alike began to push with them. These Protectors all wore the crest of the Uprising movement. Yes. At last! They had turned on their masters. Balnather's demise was coming at last. It was now just a matter of time before the door to Palace Rock was knocked down and the great flood of rioters stormed the Palace of Merthru.

Geetie turned to Naz, determination on his face. "This is it, Naz!" he called. "We're about to win!"

At last, they arrived before the gates. The defending Protectors had either fled or switched sides long ago, and so there was no longer any push back against the revolution's advancements. With a mighty *Bang!* the battering ram was slammed into the gates. It was the first strike of many.

Green Tree

Chapter Nineteen

"My father has always hated being proven wrong," said Prince Lekt.

They sat at yet another dining table, this time in one of the many gardens of Fortuna. The magical light seemed to dance around them all as they ate. Drew was still feeling relief after learning that his Kingdom had not taken Wilder Forest by force over a century before.

"You've lived like this for the past month?" Drew asked the Prince. What must living in such a magical realm be like?

The Prince shrugged. "Yes," he said. "It's been a good month, I can assure you." He saw Josh and Tenebrae staring at him in disbelief. "Well, as good as a Prince can be while his Kingdom is in a civil war," he added awkwardly.

Drew looked toward Lekt as the Prince again began telling them of what had been going on back in Boron Nigh.

"In the days before your return from Hoonth, my father was so excited," continued Lekt. "He spent his days theorising what Ker Gorûn's army could be." He looked at Drew and Tenebrae in embarrassment. "He, erm, even planned a seaside holiday in the Crownlands, once they had been defeated."

"Can you believe this guy?" asked Josh.

"So when you returned with the Ker's message, he was enraged," said Lekt. "I have never seen him so angry."

"He was proven wrong," said Duchess Wilder. "Because fighting is never the answer. Ker Gorûn's message *must* be heeded."

"I know," sighed Lekt. "The past month here has made me realise it. My father was wrong," he admitted. "Yet he still holds some form of hope that Harleland can defeat them in battle."

"It is not possible, Lekt," replied Wilder. "You are fighting two different wars. And even when the Uprising movement is crushed, will Harleland still have the strength to defeat Duke Shârvous?"

"No," whispered Lekt. He looked up, resolve in his eyes. "But I know what must be done. Once the Uprising movement is defeated, we must meet with the Crownlands and agree on a truce."

"At last, sense prevails!" called Tenebrae.

"I'll drink to that," declared Josh, downing his drink.

Drew laughed. "Wait until you're eighteen," he said. "You'll be sculling beer like there's no tomorrow!"

"And I look forward to it!" declared Josh happily.

"Oh great, a new generation of alcoholics for the Kingdom to look after," said Lekt.

"Beer isn't something I would normally scull," said Wilder. "I'm more of a wine person."

"Are you saying that you, the Duchess of Wilder Forest, scull wine?" asked Lekt, shocked.

"Yes," said Wilder matter-of-factly. "And?"

Lekt scratched his head awkwardly. Tenebrae and Josh smirked at each other.

"Now," said Wilder. "Drew, we need to talk about your vision. I need you to tell me everything you saw."

Drew nodded and began his description of the dream he had had back in Hogs. Of Queen Wilder, Elder Len, the voice of Lazarka and the seed of the Green Tree. Then he stopped. The prophecy! Lazarka had told Queen Wilder and Len of a prophecy, the very same that Ker Gorûn had told Drew before he left Hoonth.

"Gorûn said, and so did Lazarka in the vision I had, that I must seek the root that breathes green veins," explained Drew. "Gorûn didn't know what it meant… but I think it has something to do with the Green Tree."

Duchess Wilder nodded. "That prophecy has been passed down since Wilder Forest first became a Dutchy of Harleland," she said. "I think… I think you should see the seed."

Lekt looked up. "You mean, *Drew* can see the artefact?"

"So that's what Lakton wants!" said Drew. "The artefact is the seed."

"Yes," said Lekt. "The power of the Green Tree, my father thinks, could stop the Crownlands."

"Defend Harleland from the Crownlands, yes," said Wilder. "But not destroy it. This power was designed to protect and defend."

"So the seed of Lazarka," continued Drew. "It was never planted?"

"No," replied Wilder. "The seed of Lazarka was locked up in our vaults. Its power is prayed for by the Sisters of Lazarka." She pointed out the nuns in the grassy square, who Drew now recognised from his vision. "But finish your meal first, please," she finished.

Lekt shook his head impatiently. "But we need to get this seed *now*," he fretted. "The sooner we defeat the Uprising movement, the better."

"The seed is to be seen by Drew only, not the Royal Family," said Wilder. More softly, she added: "Impatience will get you nowhere, Prince Lekt. Drew, Josh and Tenebrae have had a long and hard journey to get here, and once you leave this place, it will be another hard task to then defeat the Uprising movement. Let them rest a while."

Lekt muttered to himself but did not reply to Wilder out loud.

"Well that was a merry conversation," said Josh.

They continued their meal in silence. After they had finished, Duchess Wilder rose and signalled to Drew to follow her. As Josh and Tenebrae came to follow, Wilder shook her head.

"Only Drew can see the seed," she announced.

"I understand," said Josh, though he seemed disappointed.

"Good luck!" called Tenebrae.

Lekt scowled as Wilder and Drew walked off together to the secret vault where Wilder Forest kept the seed of Lazarka safe.

***

Drew followed Duchess Wilder down a steep flight of stairs at the base of an ancient looking willow tree. The passage was dimly lit, and the musky smell of earth filled Drew's nostrils. Finally, they arrived at a door. It was wooden, but unlike any wood door Drew had ever seen. It had five ancient carvings etched into it, like runes… *Runes?!*

Drew looked at Wilder in shock. "Those aren't…"

"The Life Runes," answered Wilder. "I know what you are descended from, Saran. I know you carry the Shadow Runes with you."

Drew withdrew his rune bag. Suddenly, the five rune markings upon the door began glowing a dull green. The door opened, revealing a small dark room. In the middle of this room was a pedestal. And upon that was an inconspicuous seed. Tiny. The size that any seed would be. Wilder beckoned for Drew to follow her into the chamber.

"This is the seed of Lazarka," said Wilder. "It is said that once planted, the seed will sprout the Green Tree, and from it, will come the Life Runes."

"Wait," questioned Drew. "The Life Runes *grow* from the tree?"

"Like leaves," said Wilder. "Your Shadow Runes come from the shadows of the Ley Line that passes under Hoonth. Our Life Runes come from the branches of the Green Tree, grown in this ancient land above our own Ley Line."

Drew stared at her in wonder. "That's how my runes came to be…" he whispered. "Mined from the Hoonthish Ley Line itself!"

Wilder nodded. "Your runes have come to be," she said. "The Weather Runes of the Temple of Nearth have come to be. Yet my runes have not yet come to pass… And the Death Runes of the Indigo Tower have already faded from the world."

"Woah, slow down," said Drew. "Weather Runes too?"

He looked within his rune bag. A memory had come to him. In the bag, as well as his five rune stones, was a piece of parchment that Octavia had given him while they travelled through Dirtgula together, so long ago. The parchment displayed four lines of five runes each. His Shadow Runes were listed at the top. And the second line of runes were the same five that were inscribed upon the door to the small room he and Wilder now stood in.

"This seed must be the root that breathes green veins," said Drew. "Green veins… green shoots of life being breathed – grown – from this seed."

Wilder nodded. "I believe that is the case. In which case *you* must plant the tree, Drew."

"Me?" asked Drew. "Why?"

"The one who plants the tree wields the power of the Life Runes," explained Wilder. "You… You are one of the five! The five who are destined to save Harleland from destruction." She approached him and whispered quietly. "In order to fulfil your destiny, Andrew Saran. You must collect and master *all* the runes."

Chapter Twenty

There was a crash. Naz looked up in excitement. The gate was coming down! He looked over at his comrades, both Protectors and civilians. The battering ram was doing its job. The gate was nearly down! Finally, with one final push, the battering ram was through, the gates to Palace Rock now cleared from the path of the revolt. With a cry, Naz marched forward, Protectors in his stead as they ascended the stairs to the top of the city. The living armour that stood silently on the sides of the staircase did not move to attempt to stop the army, reinforcing into Naz once more that what he was doing was right. Although he felt somewhat upset by the state of Boron Nigh, he knew that the Uprising Inquisitors could only be removed by force.

At last, they reached the top of the stairs. The main courtyard of Palace Rock was as neat, tidy and well kept as ever. But now, it was deserted. The Palace of Merthru sat quietly before them, while the Great Hall also seemed to sleep. Naz had never seen this place so deserted before. However the peace was all over in an instant, as the army rushed into the courtyard from behind him.

"Wait!" called Naz, but it was no use.

The Protectors came in beside Naz and watched as an army of civilians and peasants stormed Palace Rock.

"This is out of control," said Sergeant Elias in alarm, the older Protector standing now beside Naz with a fresh scar down his face.

"We need to find King Lakton and Balnather at once!" said Naz. "Lakton must restore order and reclaim his powers from the Uprising movement."

Elias nodded. "Reke, Kulu, Lilthyme, with me!" he called. He saluted Naz as he and his group ran off into the chaos. "Good luck, soldier."

Naz turned to Geetie. "Up for one last adventure?" he asked.

"Of course," said Geetie. He winked.

"I'll come with you," said a new voice. It was Jemima! Naz had not seen her come up the stairs with them.

"Very well," said Naz. "Let's go."

With that, the trio ran to the Palace. Naz knew they needed to find an alternative entrance, as the main doors were being accosted by the civilian and peasant army, and were therefore blocked. Naz knew that if the army broke in and found Balnather first, the corrupt Count would surely be killed. King Lakton, too. He spotted Cron in the crowd and beckoned for him to come over.

"What's your plan now?" Cron asked.

"We need to find Balnather and Lakton before they do," replied Naz, referring to the army. "Cron, I need you to try and convince them to stand down, or at least find a way to slow them down so they can't break down that door!"

Cron nodded. "I s'pose I can do that," he responded. "Good luck. Oh, and if you do find Balnather. Give 'im a piece of me mind!" He spat the last part of his sentence, and then turned back to rejoin the rabble.

"Our revolution went too well it seems," said Geetie. "Who knows how long it will take for King Lakton to regain order around here... if he's well enough, that is." He shuddered.

Naz looked ahead darkly. "Come on," he said. "There's a back entrance to the Palace that only the Palace Rock Protectors know about. Follow me."

He led them on, rounding a corner and coming to the back of the Palace of Merthru. It was much quieter here, but the cries and jeers of the civilian and peasant army could still be heard as they tried to break down the door to the Palace.

Lucky the stairs are preventing them from bringing that battering ram up here to Palace Rock, thought Naz.

He found the secret door and looked at Jemima. She nodded in understanding.

"We need two Protectors to open the secret entrance," she explained to Geetie, who stared confused at what appeared to be a blank piece of wall.

Naz put his hand on the left of the small section of the wall, while Jemima put her hand on the right. They pushed together, and suddenly, the wall began to move backwards, and then slid to the left. A dark passage had been revealed.

"In," commanded Naz. He looked at Jemima, who seemed to hesitate, while Geetie stepped through. She had lost

Trevault, he realised again. Although unconfirmed, he had suspected they both loved each other.

"I'm sorry about Trevault," he began. "I know you two…" he trailed off.

Jemima stared at him. "Oh you stupid, daft idiot," she said. "I love *you* Naz!"

Naz's mouth dropped open. "O-oh…" he stammered.

"Trevault was one of my – *our* – best friends," she continued, tears starting to well in her eyes. "He…" She paused. "He wanted me to tell you about my feelings. Apparently, to him, it was obvious." She laughed. "Trevault was someone I could always turn to, and I loved him as a friend, and will always miss him. But I never loved him romantically." She trailed off. "Not like I do with you."

Now it all made sense in Naz's head. The stares, the blushing, on both of their parts he realised. How upset and devastated she was when he told her to keep out of his way back in Cold Valley.

"Oh, Jemima," he said, and they embraced. They would have kissed if it were not for the impatient voice of Geetie who stood still in the entrance of the secret passage.

"Hey!" he called, annoyed. "Can you save it for later?"

Naz and Jemima looked back at him awkwardly. "Oh, yeah," Naz said. "Sorry."

Jemima laughed as they both joined Geetie in the passageway and began to walk.

***

It was very dark in the passageway. It was not meant to be used for anything other than as a secret escape for the Royals if it ever came to it, but King Lakton was under such heavy surveillance from Balnather's goons that Naz reckoned he would never get the chance to use it.

Perhaps this is how Prince Lekt got out, he thought.

There seemed to be several bends in the passageway, the path snaking its way beneath the Palace of Merthru. It was very quiet in the tunnel, the angry rabble outside seemingly non-existent. He felt for Jemima's hand and squeezed it. She squeezed back.

"If we don't get out of this," she whispered. "I love you, Naz."

Naz withdrew his hand from hers, emotions coursing through him.

"I-I…" he began. "I'm sorry again, for how I spoke to you back at the valley."

"It's okay, I've already told you I forgive you," she replied. "Just… let's move forward."

He smiled, although he knew Jemima could not see it due to the darkness. "I agree," he said. "And we *will* survive. Maybe we can try and be together, after all this is over."

"Young love," said the voice of Geetie from up ahead.

Naz scratched his head awkwardly. Truthfully, he had loved Jemima, but in his belief that her heart was with Trevault, he had locked the feelings away. Now he could let them out. His heart sang at the prospect of being with her after this battle was over.

"There's light ahead!" called Geetie.

Sure enough, a faint light could be seen further up the passageway. The trio approached it, and gasped as they saw the back of the secret door that opened from the inside of the Palace into the passageway. As they had done outside, Naz and Jemima each pushed the secret buttons on each side of the door, and sure enough it swung outwards towards them. The other side of the door had a bookshelf attached to it, a perfect disguise for any secret entrance. They each stepped through and into the Palace of Merthru.

Chapter Twenty-One

The alarms rang throughout the forest, bells clanging loudly to hail the arrival of a new threat. Drew and Wilder rushed out of the vault, almost colliding with Tenebrae and Lekt as they raced to take up arms.

"What is happening?" Wilder demanded.

"Invasion!" called Lekt. "The Crownlands have sent an invasion force!"

Through the trees, Drew could make out banners, held up high by soldiers, the crest of the Crownlands borne into the fabric. Around him, the Warriors of Wilder Forest took up defensive positions. General Sylvia raced over to Duchess Wilder and ushered her Lady to somewhere safe. Tenebrae held her knife while Drew looked to Lekt and Josh.

"For Harleland," he said.

Josh nodded. Lekt, too, signalled his approval. Tenebrae held her knife above her head.

"For Harleland!" they said.

With that, Drew and Lekt unsheathed their blades, Tenebrae ran forward into the fray, while Josh withdrew his bow and notched an arrow, ready to fire. The first wave of Herks came crashing through the city, the Warriors of Wilder Forest moving to usher civilians out of harm's way. Prince Lekt gave a cry and followed Tenebrae into the battle, Drew in his stead, while an arrow from Josh whistled through the air. Drew clanged his sword against the first Herk he came across, the Crownland soldier looking at him in contempt. They parried, Drew kicking out at his assailant before being slammed in the back by another Herk. He was breathless, as he turned to swing, only to be battered once more by one of his two attackers. Suddenly one gave a cry, and Drew saw Lekt plunge his blade through the Herk soldier. Drew nodded at the Prince in thanks and turned back to his other attacker. Now the fight was fair again, one on one combat, as Drew sliced expertly at his foe, eventually wearing him down and cutting off his hand. The Herk gave a cry of pain and Drew swiftly ended his life. He was all of a sudden accosted by two more Herks, familiar looking, he realised. Irk and Murk stood before him, both teething with anger.

"You slimy little Harlelish runt!" Irk cried.

"You tricked us! Now we'll kill y'a!" said Murk.

Drew was ready for the challenge and he blocked Irk's first blow, before kicking out at Murk. He jumped back, smiling cruelly as he rushed Drew once more. Drew broke away from Irk and parried now with Murk, eventually getting the better of him as Josh fired an arrow that distracted Irk, allowing Drew to defeat his friend unimpeded. Murk lay before Drew defeated, while a Warrior parried with Irk, a Wilder Forest soldier against a Crownland soldier.

"Scram!" called Drew. "Remember my mercy."

Murk gave a cry of fear and scurried off. Drew looked around the rest of the battlefield and saw Lekt struggling against three Herks. Drew gave a cry and rushed over to the Prince, killing one of Lekt's attackers and dealing a swift blow to another who had lined up a brutal kick to the Prince.

"Thanks!" breathed Lekt as the pair went their separate ways once more.

Then Drew recognised Captain Crysthan, fighting on the other side of the battlefield. The slimy Herk leader must have led this battalion here after Tenebrae helped Drew and Josh escape from their camp back in Hogshire. He angrily made his way over to Crysthan, ready to fight the Crownland Captain. Then he stopped. He had something better in mind. The runes. He smiled darkly, the battle continuing around him. He had defeated Captain Dirk using power from the runes back at the Great Tower. Now he would defeat another Captain, using the runes once more. Drew took the bag out of his cloak and pondered. Should he use the ultimate rune again? He could wipe this entire army out.

Say it, Saran! yelled the voice in his head. *Just one word... Moarte! End these miserable runts. Free them from life. Allow them to embrace death.*

Drew began trembling. He had realised, just as the voice said 'Moarte,' that he did not want to think any of what the voice had just said. There was someone else in his mind.

"Drew!" yelled Lekt. "What are you doing?!"

Suddenly, Josh barged into Drew and tackled him, just as a Herk swung a club towards him.

"Drew!" said Josh in shock. "What in the world? You're standing there, frozen, in the middle of a battlefield! What's going on?"

"I..." stammered Drew. "I have to get out of here."

He struggled to his feet and stumbled through the battle, dodging swords, clubs and arrows, before arriving behind the safety of a large tree. He collapsed at the base of the trunk. Josh sprinted up beside him.

"What's going on?" he asked.

"The runes, they're…" said Drew, but he trailed off. He looked up at Josh in agony. "They're destroying me, Josh."

"You have to resist it Drew," said Josh. "People are counting on you!"

Drew stood shakily. Josh was right. He had to resist the voice's demands.

No! it called. *Use it, Saran! Say Moarte!*

"Never!" spat Drew.

He followed Josh back toward the fray, stumbling as he tried to recompose himself. He stopped and stood up straight. With a deep breath, Drew got himself together. Looking around he saw Tenebrae weaving between two Herks, while Lekt parried with another, and Josh stood to the side providing a steady barrage of arrows. He focused his mind. Remembering his intentions before the runes took hold, Drew scanned the battlefield once more and spotted Captain Crysthan. He unsheathed his blade and ran for the Herk Captain. Crysthan looked up in surprise as Drew accosted him. The pair parried, their clashing blades causing the sound of metal to ring out amongst the chaos of the battle. Captain Crysthan had quickly regained his composure after Drew's initial attack, and he countered with a series of swift, precise strikes. Drew fought back with vigour, and an urgency that came from his recent epiphany.

"Stand down," Crysthan demanded. His eyes narrowed. "You don't have to die for a lost cause."

Drew gritted his teeth. He would not let this Herk Captain intimidate him, even if he was still feeling the effects of shock from the mysterious rune voice.

"The only lost cause here is your blind obedience to the Crownlands," Drew retorted.

Crysthan swung at him again, but Drew pushed back with all his strength. He had to defeat this Herk Captain. He could not let Octavia and Naz down now. The battle raged around them, the pair parrying once more, while Josh fought nearby. Drew's apprentice seemed to be holding his own against two Herk soldiers, with assistance from one of Wilder Forest's Warriors. He glanced over at Drew, offering a brief nod of encouragement. Drew's resolve hardened. He shifted his stance, remembering his training, and began to fight more strategically, using his speed and agility to his advantage. He quickly ducked under a new strike from Crysthan's blade, and sidestepped as the Herk Captain tried to trip him.

Captain Crysthan, realising Drew's change in tactics, adjusted his own approach. He feigned left, then swung right, aiming for a weak spot in Drew's defence. But Drew anticipated the move, sidestepping again and bringing his blade up in a sharp arc. The edge of his sword caught Crysthan's arm, drawing a thin line of blood.

The Herk Captain hissed in pain but didn't falter. "You've got spirit," he admitted grudgingly. "But spirit alone won't save you."

"Maybe not," Drew replied, his breath coming in short, sharp gasps. "But it's a start."

Drew pressed the attack despite his rising levels of exhaustion, forcing Crysthan to take a step back. He had gained the upper hand in this fight. Suddenly, Crysthan took advantage of the position of Drew's arm, just the right height to disarm him. He lunged forward, knocking Drew's arm with a swift kick. His sword skidded across the ground and out of reach, while Crysthan took advantage of his shock and placed a brutal kick into Drew's chest. He collapsed and Crysthan stood over him, blade poised for the final blow.

"Any last words?" the Crownland soldier asked, a hint of respect in his voice.

Drew looked up, his mind racing. He had lost. Crysthan was too strong. But there was still a glimmer of hope. Something caught his eye standing just behind the Herk Captain.

"Just one," he said, a faint smile playing on his lips. "Look up."

Crysthan frowned but instinctively glanced upward. In that split second, Josh, having dispatched his opponents, leaped from behind the Herk Captain, tackling Crysthan to the ground. The two rolled, grappling fiercely, but Josh's momentum gave him the edge. He landed a solid punch to Crysthan's jaw, knocking the Herk Captain unconscious.

Josh stood, offering Drew a hand. "Nice distraction," he said with a grin.

Drew took the hand, pulling himself up. "Couldn't have done it without you," he admitted. He gazed upon his apprentice in admiration. "You saved my life, Josh," he breathed.

"Don't mention it," Josh said. "But we still have work to do."

Drew nodded. "Indeed," he said. "We have to get rid of the last of these Herks."

Together, they surveyed the battlefield. The Warriors of Wilder Forest were rallying, pushing back the Herk forces. The tide was turning, but the battle was far from over. Drew and Josh charged back into the fray, side by side, where they joined Prince Lekt and Tenebrae to try and push back the remaining Crownland forces. The Warriors joined them, the last of the Herks retreating back through the trees. The battle was over. The Warriors gave a cry of victory, Lekt and Josh joining in. But as Duchess Wilder returned from her hiding place, Drew looked at Captain Crysthan upon the ground, still alive, yet surrounded by countless dead Herks and Warriors. Intrigue washed through him. He would be a valuable prisoner for Harleland. He looked at Lekt, the Prince seeming to share his thoughts.

"We must question him when he wakes up," Lekt said.

"Agreed," said General Sylvia, as she surveyed the carnage. "Come, let us get indoors."

They carried Crysthan's unconscious form into one of the nearby buildings where he would be imprisoned for the time being. Soon they would find out the secrets of the Crownlands.

Chapter Twenty-Two

"Incredible," muttered Geetie as he, Jemima and Naz stepped into the Palace of Merthru. "Just look at the architecture in this place!"

"It's beautiful…" murmured Jemima.

Above them, the domed roof was painted with the most exquisite artwork. It displayed King Merthru the Wise, inaugural King of Harleland, touching his finger to King Merthru the Second, his son and heir. On the walls were great tapestries, emboldened with the crest of the Lakton Dynasty, however Naz noticed that some had been torn down and replaced with tapestries of the Uprising movement. Geetie had wandered in awe over to where Naz knew the Great Doctrine of Lakton was displayed in a glass casing, the document that certified the right of the Lakton Dynasty to rule over Harleland. Naz himself had been in this place many times, but he still loved the history of this Palace, and he strode over to Geetie, who had begun reading the Great Doctrine.

"By decree of the Gods of Harleland," read Geetie. "I hereby anoint Duke Lakton of the Greenarch Plain as King Lakton the First, King and Ruler of Harleland, and the head of his own Dynasty, which under the Gods, I hereby give ultimate right to rule."

"King Lakton the First was King Merthru the Second's cousin," said Naz. "The Merthru Dynasty ended and the rulership of Harleland passed to the Lakton Dynasty." He looked at Geetie. "Merthru II failed to produce an heir, and Lakton I was his closest relative."

"A fantastic history lesson," boomed a voice.

Naz and Geetie whipped around to see Balnather and another weasley looking, hunched over man standing on the other side of the room. Jemima unsheathed her blade, but Balnather continued to appear calm.

"I would not harm either me nor my fellow Inquisitor," he said. Beside Balnather, Naz recognised the weasley man was Count Hoop.

Hoop appeared much more fearful than Balnather, seeming to flinch at every bang against the door from the rabble outside.

"Balnather, perhaps we ought to just give in," he stammered. "Just hope perhaps that King Lakton will show us mercy–"

"Silence!" boomed Balnather. "Hoop, you are *weak!* Just like how Count Mossjoint is *weak!* Where is that wretch?"

"I think you'll find," started Naz. "That Mossjoint is dead."

Balnather laughed. "Oh so you killed him, did you?" He grinned. "You did me a favour then. I didn't have to do it myself."

Hoop looked at Balnather mortified. "W-why would you want a fellow Inquisitor dead?" he asked.

"Well," began Balnather. "I've realised now that three Great Leaders just wouldn't work now, would it."

Balnather suddenly lurched at Count Hoop, stabbing him in the stomach with a knife. As Naz and Jemima went to accost him, another voice could be heard.

"If you touch our Great Leader, then *yours* will die!"

Naz and Jemima stopped in their tracks and looked up. On the second level of the Palace stood General Mortimus, King Lakton in his grasp, a knife at his throat. Naz stared horrified at the King. He was frail. Very frail. He offered no resistance to Mortimus' custody of him. Balnather smiled. He strode toward the staircase that led up to the second level of the Palace.

"I have to hand it to you Naz," said Balnather from above them. "You survived the Witch of Cold Valley. Managed to raise an army to overthrow me. You would have been a valuable asset to the Uprising movement."

Naz stared in horror at Count Hoop's lifeless body before him. He realised that all power now officially rested with Balnather. The corrupt Inquisitor had always planned on killing his fellow so-called 'Great Leaders.' That had now become clear to Naz.

"So let's compromise," continued Balnather. "I will declare the Uprising movement defunct. Extinct. Dead. I'll even make you the new Chief of the Protectors!" Then he smiled. "And in exchange you will recognise me as King Balnather. A new Dynasty has begun in Harleland."

"This will be your downfall," croaked King Lakton.

"Silence!" growled Mortimus. He smacked the King around the cheek.

Naz looked up in anger. "End this now, give the King back his powers," he said. "And in exchange we shall show you mercy." He looked over at Mortimus. "Both of you."

Balnather snickered. "You forget who has the King in their custody," he said. "And... you forget who still has official control over the military."

Suddenly, the Palace door burst down. But to Naz's shock, instead of the army of civilians and peasants pouring in, it was a band of Protectors. At their head was Chief Renault.

"Get your hands off me!" called Jemima, as she was arrested.

Beside Naz, Geetie too was apprehended, followed by himself. He looked in dismay as he noticed Sergeant Elias amongst the Protectors.

"Sorry son," he said. "But Balnather is right."

Naz whipped his head around and saw Jemima, hurt plastered on her face. They had been betrayed. Geetie spat at Elias.

"You *filth!*" he screeched. "Traitorous scum!"

"I'm not the one who led a revolt," he said darkly.

Naz, Jemima and Geetie were shepherded out of the Palace. Naz stared in horror at the scene outside. The civilians, the peasants. A majority of them lay dead. Balnather and

Renault had bided their time it seemed. This was a massacre.
They were led into the Great Hall, barging past a shocked
looking Jerreter, the Royal Doorkeeper, who held the doors
of the hall open for the Uprising Protectors to herd their new
prisoners through. At the end of the hall was a cage. Naz
looked in glee as he saw Octavia. But his dismay returned
when he realised that Reke, Kulu and Lilthyme were also
locked in the cage. The three new captures were deposited
into their prison and the gate was shut with a clang. Naz
looked at Octavia and he embraced his mentor.

"Sir!" he cried. "I never thought I'd want to see someone this
badly ever again."

"Young Naz," said Octavia. "Well I never. I heard about
your deeds from Reke and the others." He looked at the
younger Protector in admiration. "Your bravery shall be
etched forevermore into the history books of Harleland."

"Thank you, sir," said Naz. He sighed. "But the revolution
has failed. We killed Count Mossjoint and Balnather killed
Count Hoop. That makes him the only Inquisitor of the
Uprising movement. He's more powerful now."

"King Balnather now," said Geetie. "I sense it is too late. A
new Dynasty of Harleland has now begun."

Lilthyme shook her head sadly. "I can't believe that Sergeant
Elias betrayed us. After all he said back in the valley…"

"An act," spat Octavia. "I always found Elias to be sneaky.
He came back to Boron Nigh after he left you all to die to the
Witch, you know."

Naz gasped.

"He informed Balnather of what had transpired, and he sent him back to ensure there were no survivors," he finished. Octavia looked over at Kulu.

"He found me on the plains, around the same time Geetie did," she said. "I trusted him, and we all went back to Cold Valley together."

Naz knew the rest. Sergeant Elias, wearing a mask for the entire trip back to Boron Nigh from Cold Valley, only to turn around and betray them all once the revolution had started.

"We can't give up now!" said Naz with purpose. "There must still be some form of hope, right?"

Jemima looked aghast. Even Geetie held a look of defeat on his usually jolly face. Balnather had scorched a mark of trauma on them all. For a second, Naz thought they had won. An army outside banging down the doors, Balnather standing defenceless just metres away from them and surrounded by two fully trained Protectors… But it all changed in an instant, and now they were all stuck in here. Octavia looked at Naz.

"There is always hope," he said. The old Protector sighed, Naz noticing in sadness his usually neatly trimmed grey beard was now an untidy grey mess.

"Drew…" whispered Geetie. "Drew is still out there."

"Yes," said Octavia. "Our hope lies now with Andrew Saran."

Chapter Twenty-Three

"What is Shârvous' next move?"

Drew and Lekt stared at Captain Crysthan, the Herk Captain kneeling before them in chains. Duchess Wilder, Tenebrae and Josh stood a little way back from the interrogation.

"Answer me!" came the angry voice of Prince Lekt.

"I would never spill my Lord's secrets!" spat Crysthan.

"Answer me this then," said Drew. "Who was the Caller who alerted you about Josh and I? Back in Hogs?"

Crysthan laughed. "We have many Callers in Hogs," he answered. "You expect me to know them all?"

"You *are* a Captain," said Lekt. He turned to Drew. "It's clearly a tactic so he doesn't rat out the Herks who live secretly in Hogs."

Drew nodded in agreement. "He'll tell us," he said. "One way or another."

"You'll have to try a bit harder then!" Crysthan chided.

"This is no use," said Wilder, as Drew and Lekt withdrew from the interrogations. "Outside of torturing him, I can't see what other information we can ascertain."

"We need to change tact then," said Lekt.

"Good news for you all, then," said the voice of General Sylvia as she walked in the room.

She was flanked by two Warriors who held a new prisoner. Drew recognised Irk.

"We found him sneaking around," Sylvia continued. "No doubt trying to rescue his master here."

Crysthan sighed. "Oh great," he muttered. "Now I'm trapped with *this* idiot."

"Sorry, sir," said Irk. "Me and Murk tried to find a way in."

"Murk?" asked Sylvia. "So there's another of you around, is there?"

Irk looked down guiltily. Crysthan rolled his eyes. Drew snickered. This dumb Herk had just given away that his friend was still outside in the city somewhere.

"Oolong, Jazmen, prepare a search party for this Murk at once!" commanded Sylvia.

The two Warriors beside her nodded and left the room. Prince Lekt approached Irk.

"And what can *you* tell us about the Crownlands plans?" asked the Prince.

"Like I'd tell you!" spat Irk. He looked over at his master. "Me and Captain Crysthan would never spill any info!"

"Crysthan and I," corrected Josh sarcastically.

By now, Lekt's anger was palpable. The Prince's face was red, and his frustration at not being able to obtain any information was showing. Angrily, he raised his hand at

Captain Crysthan. The Herk Captain showed no fear or sign of pain as Lekt brought it down upon his cheek with a mighty *Smack!*

"Prince Lekt!" called Wilder in anger. "Harming our prisoners like that makes us just as bad as them!"

Lekt looked upon the Duchess angrily. "It's war, Duchess Wilder!" he responded in annoyance. "The fate of Harleland lies in the balance. We *must* learn what Duke Shârvous' plans are."

"I think Prince Lekt is right," said Drew. "We have to get information out of them somehow, although I don't like it."

Wilder looked at Drew in anger. "You can't!" she replied. "I expected better from the prophesied saviour of Harleland. I understand this is war, but we need to be above their level!"

"With respect Duchess Wilder," said Tenebrae. "One slap cannot be considered torture."

"It's a slippery slope," replied Wilder. Defeated, she added: "So be it. But any *torturing* that takes place will not happen in Wilder Forest. You shall all have to leave."

Lekt looked at Wilder again in anger. "We have no time!" he shouted. "We have no time to determine what is moral or not! The ends justify the means, Duchess Wilder, and as your Prince I formally overrule you. We will interrogate him *here!*"

Lekt's words cast an angry and dark look over Wilder's face. With venom, she spoke to her General beside her. "General

Sylvia," said Wilder quietly, seeming to weigh up her next move carefully. "Escort them out of my forest."

Sylvia looked at her Lady in shock. "B-but, my Lady," she stammered. "The vassalage agreement signed between Wilder Forest and Boron Nigh states that the Royals have power over the Dukes and Duchesses."

"Consider the consequences of your next move very carefully," said Lekt darkly.

Drew was torn. So too, clearly, was Josh who watched on in shock.

"Then this is a test of that agreement," replied Wilder. "Sylvia, escort them off my land. That's an order!"

Sylvia looked to her and then to Lekt and Drew, as if she did not know who to listen to. Then she sighed.

"I beg for forgiveness," she said. "From you, my Lady."

Sylvia approached Wilder and bound her hands. The Duchess cried out in shock.

"This is treason, General Sylvia!" she shouted, as she was taken away.

Prince Lekt looked after the General. "Thank you," he said. He turned to Drew. "The interrogation can now continue."

Sylvia escorted Wilder out of the room, while Drew turned to Josh conflicted.

"Sylvia arrested her own Duchess!" he cried. He turned to Lekt. "What now?"

Lekt shook his head. "This was not what I wanted," he said. "But if she is going to interfere in the interrogation, then we have no choice but to get Wilder out of our way." He approached Crysthan and withdrew a knife. "I'll ask you again," said the Prince menacingly. "What is Shârvous' next move?"

"What will you do?" asked Crysthan, almost humorously. "Cut an ear off each time I refuse to answer. Slice off a finger?"

Lekt bore down upon Crysthan in anger, slicing off his thumb. Blood sprayed from the stump where it once grew. The Herk Captain cried out in pain, but still stared defiantly at Prince Lekt.

"Answer me!" yelled the Prince. "What is Shârvous' next move!?"

"Cut them all off!" screamed Crysthan. "I'll never tell you! I would never betray the Crownlands!"

Tenebrae left the room, unable to watch the scene in front of her, while Lekt almost did as Crysthan had dared, slicing off three more fingers from the left hand of the Herk Captain, stopping to try and interrogate the Herk Captain further.

"You think I'm joking with you!?" cried the Prince.

Crysthan smiled. "You would make a good Herk," he replied.

Prince Lekt looked upon the Herk Captain. "Never!" he said. "I'd never be like you."

He moved back to where Drew and Josh watched on.

"I'll tell you," said the voice of Irk suddenly.

"No!" cried Crysthan. "I demand you, no!"

Drew looked at Lekt. "I'll handle this one," he said. He approached Irk. "Tell me."

"Duke Shârvous wanted more wood to fuel the forges of the Black Fortress, back in Crown's Crossing," explained Irk.

Crysthan looked at his charge in anger, but said nothing.

"We've been felling the trees in the north of Wilder Forest for years, but…" he trailed off. "My Lord wished to obtain *better* fuel. They say that wood harvested from the city of Fortuna burns forever. He wishes to wipe out the army of Wilder Forest and use the entire Dutchy as his own personal fuel source."

Drew looked at Lekt and Josh in horror. The Prince held a grave look upon his face, while Josh was staring at Irk wide eyed.

"Then the Crownlands will have enough fuel to forge weapons forevermore, enough to destroy Boron Nigh and take over Harleland once and for all!" finished Irk.

Drew, Lekt and Josh huddled around and whispered to each other quietly.

"How in my father's name can we negotiate a truce with an army whose plan is *that?*" asked Lekt.

Drew shook his head. For the first time, he held doubts about Ker Gorûn's request. Was his grandfather wrong?

Lekt approached Crysthan. He looked upon the injuries he had inflicted upon the Herk Captain. "I respect you," he began. "I shall offer you medical assistance, and then the freedom to return to the Crownlands."

Crysthan said nothing, but he was clearly in pain and was trying his best not to show it.

"And what about me?" asked Irk.

Lekt shook his head. "Your life is in danger now," he said. "Once your Lord finds out that you told us of his plans, there is no telling what he would do to you."

Crysthan remained silent, while Irk wept. "I'll never be able to go home now…" he said. "What have I done?"

Lekt looked at Drew surely, as Josh addressed the crying Crownland soldier.

"You've just helped us achieve peace," he said. "For both of us."

Chapter Twenty-Four

As Naz lay in the cage, he dreamed of freedom. Two days had passed since he, Geetie and Jemima had been captured by Balnather. It seemed like longer. They were fed twice a day by their guards, some slop that one would expect to find in a prison. He and Jemima slept hand in hand, hope fading each passing hour. Octavia was always quick to point out that Drew was still out there, with Josh, and maybe even Prince Lekt, if they had found him by now.

"And then Lekt will come back, defeat Balnather, and assist his father with regaining the throne," the former Chief of the Protectors said.

"Let's hope so," whispered Geetie. "The quest to save Harleland from the Crownlands seems doomed though. Even if King Lakton returns to power, what if he continues to ignore Ker Gorûn's message?"

Octavia shook his head. "Somehow, I don't think Prince Lekt would allow him."

"And what about Josh?" asked the merchant, clearly worried about his son. "I hope he's okay… I know Drew will protect him. But still, I'm worried he'll be rounded up and thrown in here too."

Naz looked over at Octavia. While Geetie was concerned for his family, Octavia had not said much about his. Naz's own parents still lived in his home Dutchy of Cernsland and as far as he knew were safe from the reaches of the Uprising movement for now.

"How's your wife going through all this, Octavia?" he asked.

"She's safe," answered the old Protector. "That's all that matters. But I miss her."

"Her name is Summer, right?" asked Geetie. "You spoke about her, back in Cold Valley when we passed through."

"I did," sighed Octavia. He looked at Geetie in sadness. "I haven't seen her in months. I didn't think it would be safe when I got back from the Great Tower." He looked at Naz. "She's in Cernsland too. I convinced her to go there before I left for Hoonth with Drew."

"I wish to return there myself, when all this is over," admitted Naz. "I miss my home."

The beauty of the coastline of Cernsland was unmatched, in Naz's opinion. It had quaint villages and open hearted people, and just an overall sense of home. Far enough away from Boron Nigh to be free of the political infighting, yet still a proud Dutchy of Harleland. He had hoped to be posted there, but the promise given to him by Octavia had been shattered by the rise of Renault as the new Chief of the Protectors following the Uprising movement coming to power.

Naz looked over at Jemima. "What about your family?" he asked.

"My mother and younger sister live in the East Bay of Boron Nigh," she replied. "They've been locking themselves away since Balnather and the Uprising Inquisitors took control. They're both safe for now, thankfully." She sighed in relief.

"For your family, we will put this right," announced Octavia. "They can walk free again." He sighed. "One day."

Naz fidgeted. He hoped Octavia was right. For now, there was nothing any of them could do but hope for a miracle.

***

"Tell me!" Balnather screamed.

Beside him, Chief Renault held a whip. The Chief of the Protectors cracked it upon Naz's back. He gave a cry of pain.

"What was the little scheme you and Octavia had going back at that miserable orphanage?" Balnather asked.

Naz was tied up, shirtless, facing away from Count Balnather and Renault. Marlo had come from Dempair at Balnather's command and stood beside them. It appeared that Octavia had admitted to the Inquisitor that he, Drew and the others had been conspiring against him, and Marlo was fueling the fire.

"I saw them whispering whenever I wasn't looking," she said. "That miserable old fool Octavia and Saran. That Gunnersbury boy as well! Ha!" she laughed. "He thinks he can become a great man like his father."

"Geetie Gunnersbury has also fallen," said Balnather. "A fool. Throwing away the good life he and his son had to help this revolution."

"Indeed, Great Leader!" agreed Marlo.

"That is *King* to you!" Balnather screamed, causing Marlo to flinch. He turned his attention back to Naz. "Now. Tell us! What did you and Octavia talk about in those meetings you had behind the Palace!"

"W-we…" stammered Naz. "We exchanged information! I told him what was happening at Palace Rock, and he told me what was happening in Dempair."

"Who else from Palace Rock was in on this?" Balnather asked.

"No one," said Naz, but he was whipped once more by Renault as Balnather screamed his disapproval at his answer. "I swear!" cried Naz, tears welling up in his eyes from the pain. He turned his head to try and look at his back and to his horror saw three massive red scars criss crossing each other. "I didn't tell anyone else, no one else was in on it, because Octavia and I didn't know who we could trust!"

"Octavia *did* say the same thing, my Lord," said Renault. "I think he's telling the truth."

"So be it," spat Balnather. He turned to Renault. "Saran still has not returned from his mission. The little *oaf* must have abandoned his post."

"Perhaps his friends have heard from him?" suggested Marlo. "What about that Tenebrae girl?"

"We've searched for her," growled Renault. "We searched the orphanage in Dempair up and down. It appears she's just vanished without a trace."

"No doubt she joined Saran and the younger Gunnersbury on their quest," said Balnather. "A pity. I hoped that Andrew Saran would become an important member of my administration. His runes would come in handy."

"How did you know about the runes?" asked Naz in shock.

"Because your Petty King Lakton told me, that's why!" crowed Balnather. "How Saran possesses magic stones that could uphold my rule forever, and ensure my dynasty remains even after I am gone!"

"He'd never join you!" Naz spat.

"Don't be so sure," said Balnather. "I also understand that using the runes comes with… side effects." Naz could not see him, but he knew that Balnather had a cruel smile on his face as he said that. "Thank you, Naz," continued Balnather. "Your punishment is concluded, for now. Take him back to his cage!"

Renault and Marlo untied Naz and led him back to the prison where Octavia and the others awaited. Jemima stared in horror when she saw the injuries on Naz's back as he was tossed back into the cell.

"Oh, no!" she called. "Please, Chief Renault! He needs medical attention!"

Renault looked at her. Was that conflict in his eyes? "King Balnather would not allow it," he said finally. "I am sorry."

With that, he and Marlo walked away.

"Easy now, Naz," said Octavia. "Rest on your stomach for the time being. The pain will take some time to subside."

Jemima looked up at him. "D-did they whip you, too?" she asked.

Octavia nodded. "Until they got what they wanted out of me," he said. "Information about our revolution plans."

"How many lashings?" asked Geetie.

Octavia looked distant, as if remembering a past trauma. "Six," he said.

"Are you okay?" the merchant asked.

Outside, there was a change of guards, two new Protectors coming to guard the prisoners.

"I am now," replied Octavia. He sighed. "I am now."

"Ha!" came a laugh from one of the new guards.

They looked out and saw him laughing at them.

"I reckon he must have been crying in there for days!" he said again.

"Don't belittle him, you filth!" cried Jemima.

"Hey, maybe we should go in there and make him cry some more!" said the guard.

His fellow guard looked at him unsure. "Erm," he said. "Isn't our job just to guard the cage?"

"Oh, don't be a party pooper!" said the original guard. "Let's just open the cage and, I don't know, torture them."

Naz was taken aback by the guard's cruelty. Who in the hell did he think he was? Octavia also looked confused.

"Cruel mites!" called Geetie. "I expect more civility from the Herks of the Crownlands!"

"Well, okay, if you say so," said the other guard, still unsure.

He took out his keys and unlocked the gate. Suddenly, the original guard kicked at him. Immediately, Octavia sprung into action and tackled the second guard. Naz and the others all looked up in shock as the original guard took off his helmet. It was Cron.

Chapter Twenty-Five

The moors of Cernsland lay off to the left, the Greenarch Plain to the right, while directly before them sat the Crownlands, brooding and quiet in the early morning moonlight. A small stone monument a few metres away marked the meeting point of the three borders. Drew, Tenebrae and Lekt had accompanied Crysthan out of Wilder Forest and along the boundary between Cernsland and the Greenarch Plain to the border with the Crownlands. They had been shocked not to have encountered any Herks on their journey north-east, however Crysthan had told them it was likely their forces had been pulled out of Wilder Forest for now after the failed attack on Fortuna. Prince Lekt unbound the wrists of Captain Crysthan and stood back from him.

"Go back to your homeland," he declared. "Let my mercy towards you be a turning point in this war."

"Thank you," replied Crysthan dryly, looking upon his bandaged hand. "But I have one final request. Please ensure Irk is afforded the best possible life."

"I will do what I can," said Lekt.

With that, Crysthan crossed back into the Crownlands. Drew and Lekt watched him go, the figure of the Herk Captain getting smaller and smaller as he travelled further away.

"It seems so… similar," said Tenebrae, from behind them. "The Crownlands, I mean."

Lekt sighed. "It's similar because it's the same country," he said. "There is more in common between us and them then either of us know."

"What do we do now?" asked Drew. "Duchess Wilder won't be pleased about getting overruled back there."

"I fear the relationship between myself and Wilder Forest is now irreparably damaged," admitted Lekt. "But I had to do what I had to do. And Irk's confession proved me right."

Drew had no response, nor did Tenebrae, and the trio walked back towards Wilder Forest.

As Lekt walked on ahead, Drew looked over at Tenebrae. He realised with a jolt that they had not had any time together these past months. Inwardly, he felt a great deal of sadness. At one point, Drew had harboured feelings for her. But so much had changed, and he was unsure of where their relationship stood.

"I've missed you, Tenebrae," Drew said, finding the words at last.

Tenebrae looked ahead. "I have too, Drew," she replied. "I'm glad we're still able to see each other despite everything that's happened."

"I..." Drew began, but he trailed off. He felt nervous about admitting his feelings. "I just wanted you to know, that... Back in Dirtgula, just after we first met, I started to like you. A lot."

Tenebrae did not look at him, and they kept walking.

"But I wanted you to know that the feelings I had for you – romantically – are gone. But I want to be friends. You, Josh, Geetie, Octavia – you four are my world, Tenebrae."

It felt like a great weight had just lifted off from his shoulders. He was free of his bottled up emotions at last. Tenebrae looked over at him and stopped, and she smiled.

"Thanks for telling me, Drew," she replied. "I think I liked you too, but… I don't think it would work either, and I'm glad we're on the same page with our relationship."

The pair walked onwards together in silence, still a good fifteen meters or so behind Prince Lekt, as the morning sun began to rise, and the trees of Wilder Forest came closer and closer.

***

Upon their arrival back in Fortuna, General Sylvia had come rushing out of the Palace to meet them. Josh stood to the side, waiting for Drew and Tenebrae's update.

"My Prince," Sylvia said, bowing to Lekt. "I strongly advise a meeting with my Duchess."

"That is what I have in mind," replied Lekt. He turned to Drew and Tenebrae. "I shall speak to Wilder privately. Await me out here."

With that, he turned and followed Sylvia to the Duchess's Chambers, high up in the ancient tree Palace. Josh approached Drew and Tenebrae in concern.

"I don't like this," he admitted. "Something doesn't feel right."

"I agree," replied Tenebrae. "It's just the way that Lekt undermined Duchess Wilder's authority in her own Dutchy."

"I know," replied Drew. "I don't like it either. But Lekt had to do what he thought was right." He paused. "But there's something else as well. I'm worried about what's going on back in Boron Nigh."

"Do you think Octavia is still imprisoned?" asked Josh.

"It wouldn't surprise me," said Drew darkly. "I would think Balnather would keep him heavily guarded at all times." He sighed. "If only Naz hadn't been sent off to Cold Valley, I'm sure he could've done something."

As they spoke, the Sisters of Lazarka had begun their daily ritual on the grassy square nearby the Palace. Drew looked over and observed in wonder. The nuns, seven of them, had begun to chant.

Glory to Lazarka, our gracious giver of life.

Glory to Lazarka, she who breathes green veins.

The head of the order now took her place at the front of the ritual as Drew, Josh and Tenebrae watched on.

"We, the keepers of Lazarka's will, do bless her," she said. "We pay homage to her Ley Line that runs beneath us, we pay homage to all that gives life, the seed of Lazarka and the spirit of the Sisters of Lazarka, and the gracious gifts that are imparted upon us all!"

The rest of the nuns repeated her statement, their chanting echoing through the treetops around Fortuna, filling Drew's ears with wonder. The nuns now danced, a strange formation it appeared to Drew, but to the locals who had come by to watch the ritual also, a very sacred and holy sight.

"This is why Duchess Wilder seems so independent," said Josh in amazement. "She wants to protect this from being erased. From becoming a gentrified part of Harleland like Hogshire, or Lekt Valley."

Drew nodded. "The ancient Queens of Wilder Forest didn't seem keen to become vassals of King Merthru," he said. "This is… special."

As the ritual came to its close, Drew was surprised to see the head of the order approaching him. She held a warm smile upon her face. She greeted them with a bow.

"You must be Andrew Saran," she began, before turning to the others. "And Josh Gunnersbury and Tenebrae." She addressed them all now. "I am the Eldest Sister, head of the Sisters of Lazarka."

"That's your full name?" asked Josh.

The Eldest Sister laughed. "Yes, young Josh," she replied. "Upon receiving the honour of leading the order, one must give up their name. It is the same as the Duchesses of Wilder Forest."

"They must all take the name Wilder," Tenebrae explained, looking at Josh.

"That makes sense now," he replied.

"Andrew Saran," said the Eldest Sister. "You are the centre of the prophecy of the Green Tree. It is for that reason I wanted to speak to you in person. I sense there is something within you. Something that has not seen this world in many ages."

Drew looked at her in alarm. "What is in me?" he asked.

"First you must take up the seed of Lazarka," the Eldest Sister continued, ignoring him. "Plant it, and obtain the Life Runes from the Green Tree that grows from it."

"Andrew!"

The voice of Prince Lekt came from the entrance to the Palace, someway off.

"Duchess Wilder will speak to you now," he called again.

"Thank you, Andrew Saran," said the Eldest Sister. "I will always remember speaking with you."

She wandered back to the grassy square with the other nuns, the seven Sisters of Lazarka returning to their monastery, supposedly built on the outskirts of the city. An old man approached Drew. He held a look of wonder on his face.

"In all my long years," he croaked. "Never have I seen the Eldest Sister speak with an audience member."

Drew looked back in amazement before turning toward Lekt. He strode over to the Palace entrance, nodding at the Prince as he entered. He ascended the stairs, gazing once again at the glowing insects that provided the pale green light that lit up the inside of the trunk. He arrived once more in Duchess Wilder's quarters, the Lady of Wilder Forest sitting on a chair on her balcony, watching over the grassy square. She turned and beckoned for Drew to enter.

"I witnessed what just happened," she said. "Drew, I do not agree with Prince Lekt's methods. I do not like what he did in undermining my authority. However, for the greater good, I shall look past that for now." She gazed at him. "Hold out your hand."

Drew took a step forward and did as she asked, his palm before Wilder, facing up. In it, she deposited the small seed of Lazarka. She must have taken it from the vault before the invasion, keeping it safe until the right moment to hand it over to Drew.

"You must plant this, Drew," she whispered. "Plant the seed, and from the Green Tree, take the Life Runes, and master them."

Drew nodded. "I won't let you down," he said. "I will never forget the trust you have placed in me."

He descended from Wilder's Palace, Lekt and Josh joining him as he searched for a spare patch of earth to plant the seed of Lazarka. Tenebrae was right by his side as he searched for the perfect place. Each part of Fortuna seemed to be full of beautiful, lush plants and trees, and the areas that were not were covered in soft grass. Then he saw it. The only place within the city he could find with a vacant patch of brown soil. It was an unassuming spot, just next to an apple tree, and in the shadow of a regular house. He knelt down. And as he inserted the seed into the soil, he immediately saw green light glowing from the small hole. He stood back, and all present watched in wonder as green shoots of light, vein-like in appearance shot from the new roots beneath the surface, forming a beautiful tree with five branches. And upon those five branches, growing like leaves, were five brand new runes.

Chapter Twenty-Six

Naz threw Jemima a sword, while Octavia brandished his own blade found in the King's armoury. Cron still had the weapon he had found with the guard's armour he had stolen, while Geetie, Reke, Kulu and Lilthyme held a short sword each.

"We need to find King Lakton," said Naz. "Search every room in the Great Hall and the Palace to find where Balnather is keeping him." He stopped suddenly and stared at Octavia guiltily. "Sorry," he muttered. "With your permission, sir."

Octavia beamed with pride. "No, Naz," he said. "This is your mission. You are in charge here, *sir*."

Jemima looked at Naz proudly. He himself felt a wave of happiness and confidence course through him. For Octavia to rescind command to him! What an honour!

"Then we shall split up and search for Lakton," he commanded. "Octavia and Geetie will search the rest of the Great Hall. Kulu and Reke, search around the outside. Cron and Lilthyme, I want you two to help Jemima and I to search the rooms of the Palace."

"Of course," said Lilthyme. "Let's go."

"We all meet back in the main room of the Palace of Merthru in thirty minutes," continued Naz. "And remember – once we have Lakton in our care, then Balnather loses any bargaining power he has."

"Okay, let's do it," agreed Octavia. "With me Geetie!"

"Oh, another Geetie and Octavia adventure!" called Geetie in excitement, as the others broke off into their pairs.

It was night outside, and Naz, Jemima, Cron and Lilthyme said their farewells to Kulu and Reke as they swept off into the darkness of the courtyard. Naz looked upon the Palace of Merthru once again. The main doors were still ruined after Renault and his Protectors barged them down days ago to storm Naz and his friends when they had originally arrived in the Palace. There were guards posted, however Jemima and Lilthyme expertly snuck up behind them both, silently downing them.

"Okay, the coast is clear!" whispered Lilthyme with urgency.

The four snuck into the dark Palace, before splitting off to search the dark rooms for Lakton. Naz and Jemima ran upstairs, allowing Cron and Lilthyme to search below. They walked into a library, candles still burning on the walls around them, allowing the duo to see their way around the room.

"King Lakton has quite the collection," breathed Jemima. She picked out an old novel from one bookshelf and dusted it off. She smiled. "My father used to read this to me when I was young," she said. "It's a true story, about a man named Arthur who fought a dragon!"

Naz looked at the book. He smiled at her. He was glad the books made her happy.

"There was one book my mother read to me," he said. "It was a silly tale, a little girl went down a rabbit hole and into a magic Kingdom!"

Jemima laughed. "I remember that one!" she said. "Oh let's see, there was another one, about a man who flew around in a blue box, of all things!"

"Yes, that does sound intriguing!" laughed Naz. He stared at her now, their eyes boring into each other.

"Perhaps..." said Jemima. "We could read these books together." She shook her head, almost like an intrusive thought had slipped out.

Naz gulped, before changing the subject quickly. "W-we'd better search another room," he said awkwardly.

"Oh, yes," stammered Jemima. "O-of course."

They recomposed themselves and left the library. The next room along did not grant them the luxuries of candlelight, only the stars glittering from out the window allowing them to see at all. But then Naz's heart froze. He heard snoring. To his horror, he could just make out the sleeping figure of Chief Renault. He quickly motioned to Jemima, who stopped dead in her tracks. Slowly, very slowly, the pair began to back away. A creak sounded as Naz placed his foot down on an old floorboard. He cringed and screwed his eyes shut. After pausing for a moment, they continued their slow reverse until finally they were out of the room. They poked their heads in the next room, much more cautious this time around. No one. Jemima laughed in relief, Naz joining her. It was dark in this room to, but the moonlight allowed Naz to see Jemima's eyes again. Once more, they were staring at each other, and without realising it, had begun to move closer. Suddenly they embraced, kissing passionately as if it would be the last thing they would ever do. Naz came to just in time to stop himself from tearing off Jemima's clothing. He broke away from the kiss and looked at her, her eyes the most beautiful thing he had ever seen.

"I-I'm sorry," he stammered.

"I want you," Jemima breathed, shooshing him.

"Oh?" replied Naz in confusion. "Wait." He comprehended what she meant.

He could just make out her eyes rolling, and a huge grin on her face. They pulled away from each other and Jemima reorganised her hair. "We'll continue that later," she said.

Naz nodded. "Count me in," he said.

They left the room and went into the next, Naz feeling huge waves of confidence coursing through him, like he could take on the entire world. Into the room they went, carefully, and saw a giant map on a table in the middle. Cartography stands lined the walls. And a candle gave off enough light to allow them to see a guard standing by a bed. Naz and Jemima pressed against the wall. The guard appeared tired, yet he immediately perked up when he noticed someone enter the room. He looked around.

"Show yourselves!" he said defiantly. "You're not some of those peasants from down below?"

Then, from the bed, came the weak voice of King Lakton.

"Come for me, maybe," it croaked. "Yes. Hmm…"

Naz whispered into Jemima's ear. "We could easily take him!"

"But he'll alert Renault!" she protested. "He's just two rooms down, remember?"

"And when we have King Lakton, what will Renault do?" asked Naz.

"Naz, did you not see the way he looked when he locked us away the other day?" she asked. "I think he's seriously questioning Balnather and the Uprising movement." She paused. "And… well, what about his brother? I don't think he'd even know that Trevault is dead."

Naz breathed. "Fine!" he whispered.

Adrenaline rushed through him. This was it. He and Jemima held each other's hands and leaped out of the shadows together, bearing down upon the guard. He gave a cry, his shout echoing throughout the Palace, waking all within it for sure. Naz used the hilt of his sword to render the guard unconscious and stood now before King Lakton. He was so frail, Naz realised with shock. The once Kingly figure now appeared as a skinny old man, hunched before them.

"Oh…" he said. "Naz! Yes…" He coughed.

At that moment, shouting could be heard down the corridor. Naz and Jemima helped the weak King to his feet and rushed out of the room. As Naz had ordered, the others were waiting for them downstairs. Renault and a handful of other Uprising Protectors stormed after them, gazing at Naz and Jemima in shock.

"They have escaped!" he cried.

Naz, Jemima and Lakton ran down the stairs to where Octavia and the others stood in the middle of the entrance hall, beneath the great domed roof.

"You are safe now, my King," stated Octavia, as he assisted Lakton to stand.

"Octavia…" said the King, confused. "Yes, my friend. I dreamt that I demoted you as my Chief of the Protectors… I don't know…"

Octavia stared at Renault defiantly. "You have lost!" he called.

He took a step forward. Renault unsheathed his blade and motioned to his Protectors to stay back.

"I am doing my duty!" he cried. "Do you not think it pains me to betray our King? Of course it does! But the charter of the Protectors states that we serve whoever is legally in charge, and as it stands, that is Balnather!"

"So be it," said Octavia.

Hence, the battle began. Octavia parried with Renault, the pair striking each other with their blades, the two most experienced and battle hardened Protectors in Harleland

engaging in a most intense duel. Naz went to help his
mentor, but he was held back by Geetie.

"Wait," said the merchant.

Naz instead watched on at the battle before them. Octavia
feigned right and took advantage of Renault as he fell for the
trick, slamming the hilt of his sword into the Chief's ribs.
Renault gave a cry of pain and kicked at Octavia. He
stumbled backwards, but recomposed himself and swung his
blade back at Renault. The Chief blocked the blows before
pulling his own trick, feigning right before sidestepping a
blow from Octavia and slicing his blade along the former
Chief's cheek. Blood poured from the wound upon his face,
yet Octavia seemed to feel no pain as he stared back at
Renault.

"End this madness!" he cried. "Withdraw your support from
Balnather! Help Harleland rebuild, and we can finally focus
on brokering peace with the Crownlands!"

"Never!" spat Renault.

He lunged for Octavia and his sword found its mark,
piercing the former Chief's left shoulder. Octavia gave a
blood curdling cry. He sank to his knees. The blade had
embedded itself so deep within his shoulder that Renault
could not dislodge it. He looked in fear at Naz, who bore
down upon him with anger, striking Renault with his blade.
Blood splattered all over the floor, the Chief of the
Protectors sinking to his knees before Naz who put his sword
to Renault's throat. At once, Geetie and Jemima ran over to
Octavia who continued to bleed out beside them.

"Trevault is dead," Naz declared, looking into Renault's eyes. "Your brother paid the ultimate price for your treachery."

Pain came across Renault's face. "I never wanted any of this," he said. "I did what I thought was right! The code of the Protectors! Lakton officially signed command over to Balnather and the Inquisitors!"

"And Balnather killed one of the Inquisitors himself!" yelled Naz. "All to ensure his own power."

Behind Renault, the Uprising Protectors dropped their weapons, clearly making up their own minds. Renault looked up at Naz, unable to speak. Finally, he conceded.

"I surrender."

Chapter Twenty-Seven

Drew gazed in wonder at the Green Tree. It was not mighty by any means. It appeared the same size as a small apple tree, its five branches extending outward with the runes etched into the green leaves that sprouted from them. As he approached it, the branches hung down, extending out toward him as if offering the new runes to him. Drew grasped his hand around one leaf and pulled it off the branch. The magical light that seemed to illuminate it seemed to die, and the branch retreated, appearing now as normal wood. The other four branches had extended toward him also, and he picked the remaining four leaves from them, those branches also retreating back and losing their light. Now, with all five runes picked, the Green Tree sat as a normal tree, its magical purpose fulfilled. Drew gazed upon the five new runes, white markings etched into the green leaves. These were the Life Runes, and they read as follows:

"What spells do they cast?" asked Josh, approaching Drew in wonder.

Drew picked out the first Life Rune and read its translation out loud.

Protect.

At once, a forcefield manifested itself around Drew and Josh. They stared at it in wonder, a barely visible bubble enveloping the two Protectors. From outside, Tenebrae looked on in wonder. Drew already knew that it would deflect any attack just by looking at it. He closed his hand around the rune, ending the spell, and the protective bubble disappeared.

"The Life Runes are designed to protect and heal, not attack and inflict," said Duchess Wilder, approaching them. "They are the opposite to the Shadow Runes in that regard."

Drew nodded in understanding. "Duchess Wilder, this is the greatest gift you could have given," he said. "I am forever grateful."

She smiled. "You now have the tools to continue your task," she said. "I recommend that you return now to Boron Nigh." She stared at Lekt. "All of you."

"But–" started Lekt.

"You have what you came here for, Prince Lekt," Wilder explained. "Just not in the way you were expecting."

Lekt looked at Drew. "Well, Saran," he said. "We're counting on you. My father and I, nay, our entire Kingdom, is counting on you."

"I understand," he said. "Let us go. We must return to Boron Nigh as quickly as possible."

"Lekt's ends have indeed justified his means," said Wilder. "However the relationship between myself and the Crown will be forever shaken." She sighed. "I wish you luck."

Drew nodded, and he joined Lekt, Tenebrae and Josh as they made their way out of the city of Fortuna. Inwardly he felt doubt. Could he master these new runes in such a short amount of time? He still did not fully understand the Shadow Runes, yet something about the Life Runes felt different. It was like a gentle voice, softly giving Drew words of encouragement.

The company were escorted through the forest by General Sylvia, who gazed ahead with purpose. They all walked silently along the main road back towards the exit to the forest. Drew breathed in the fresh forest air. He had grown so used to it, he wondered how he would ever adjust to the atmosphere outside. He recognised some of the landmarks he had passed on his way to the city, the bird bath and the second gate, several large trunks that lay just off the path, and beautiful sparkling streams that no doubt held the freshest water in Harleland. After over an hour, they arrived back at the main entrance to Wilder Forest. Drew looked out at Hogshire once again, its capital of Hogs in the distance, and behind that, blue on the horizon, the Harlelish capital city of Boron Nigh. The guards by the gate nodded at them as the trio passed through, Sylvia remaining behind the gate in her own Dutchy.

"Farewell," she said. "I hope we can meet again someday."

Drew nodded back. "Thank you for your hospitality," he said.

"I shall certainly travel back here," said Tenebrae.

Josh thanked Sylvia also, while Lekt gazed at her in respect.

"I put you in an awful position the other day," he said. "I am sorry."

"You did what had to be done," replied Sylvia. "My task now is to convince my Lady that what I did was in the Kingdom's best interests."

"I wish you luck," replied Lekt. He sniffed. "We had better move. It's getting cold out. We must get to Hogs by nightfall."

"And hopefully we don't get caught out by any Callers this time," said Josh.

"Even if we do, I'll be here to save you again," smirked Tenebrae.

"Oh that *does* make me feel better!" said Josh with a smirk.

They began to walk. Drew looked back at the forest. The two guards stood stoically by the gate, while General Sylvia waved in farewell, before turning back and disappearing into the forest.

"There is one problem," said Drew. "Murk. Sylvia said they couldn't find him."

"A simple-minded fool," said Lekt. "If he's anything like Irk, then he won't be much of a threat."

Drew wanted to agree but he still felt uneasy. They trudged onward along the road, the green hills of Hogshire surrounding them on all sides as they pressed closer to their next destination.

"This is really something," said Drew happily, looking out over the landscape.

Lekt nodded. "Hogshire is one of Harleland's hidden gems," he said. "But my father used it as a dumping ground for refugees who had fled here from over the sea in Belrance."

Drew remained silent. He could put up with Lekt sometimes, but for now he could think of better things to do than engage in a political debate about refugees. They continued on in silence, halting every now and then to rest. The sun crept ever lower, eventually setting as the company finally arrived into the town. Drew and Josh had returned to Hogs, and now was the time to find accommodation for the evening. They decided it was safer to avoid the inn where they had stayed previously due to Drew's suspicions that the Herk Caller who had ratted he and Josh out to Crysthan was one of the bar staff. They settled upon a cosy looking place, *The Squire's Gambit* it was called, and Drew gazed longingly at the beer barrels behind the bar. Lekt, meanwhile, had covered himself with his cape to avoid being recognised. He handed Drew some money.

"Pay for the room," he said. "I shall head straight up there, to avoid being seen."

Drew nodded, and he and Josh approached the bar and purchased the room.

"You ain't part of that Uprising group, are y'a?" asked the bartender.

"Oh, uh," stammered Drew. Unsure of whether it was a test or not, he replied: "I just want to pay for a room, not get involved in politics."

"You ain't local I assume?" asked the bartender.

"Well, we *are* staying in a hotel," Tenebrae pointed out.

Josh nodded in agreement.

The barman looked at them both in displeasure as Drew paid the money and bought a drink. They sat together in the corner.

"Why so suspicious of the Uprising movement around here?" asked Drew, as they took their seats.

Tenebrae shrugged. "Maybe they've got more influence now in Hogs compared to last time," she suggested.

Drew sipped at his beer. He sighed in bliss. He had been craving another Hogshire Brew, and this was certainly hitting the spot. But worry still gnawed him. If things in Hogs were beginning to deteriorate, what state would Boron Nigh be in when they finally returned?

***

The gates of Boron Nigh sat open as the Prince returned. It was early morning when Drew, Josh and Tenebrae followed him into the city and stared around in shock. Civilians silently went about their day, not one of them talking to each other. The buildings were smashed, windows broken, and traces of several fires appeared to show throughout the capital.

"What happened here?" asked Lekt.

"A revolution," said Drew. "Someone got sick of the Uprising movement.

Their shock was magnified when they came to the gates of Palace Rock. They had been destroyed and the battering ram of Boron Nigh sat discarded next to them. The East Bay Protector Unit was devoid of Protectors and appeared to have been taken up by squatters.

"Oh great," said Lekt. "They'll be a pain to get out."

The trio climbed up the staircase, past the living suits of armour and into the main square of Palace Rock, where they heard a commotion coming from within the Palace of Merthru. They ran over and looked inside just in time to see Naz standing over Chief Renault. Drew gasped as he heard Renault declare his surrender. Was that it? Had they won?

Chapter Twenty-Eight

"Bravo!" called King Lakton.

He hobbled weakly over to Naz, but to his shock, the King walked straight past everyone. Naz turned back in surprise. There, standing at the entrance to the Palace, was Andrew Saran, Josh Gunnersbury, Tenebrae and Prince Lekt. The heir of Harleland ran over to his father and grabbed him as he lost his balance and nearly fell.

"Father!" he cried as Lakton fell to the floor.

Geetie got up from tending to Octavia and raced over to his son. "Josh!" he cried in relief.

"I'm okay, Dad," said Josh, but he could not help but laugh as Geetie smothered him.

Naz approached Drew and nodded at him in greeting. "It is good to see you again," he said.

"And you," replied Drew. "But what in the world has happened? And you're supposed to be dead."

"I'm sure I'll be able to tell you all about the witch incident someday," said Naz.

"Well, Josh, Tenebrae and I have had some adventures of our own," he replied. "But for now, I see that Renault had admitted defeat?"

The Chief of the Protectors knelt defeated still. He had been bound by Kulu and Reke, who stood watching over him.

"Where is Balnather?" Naz asked.

"He slithered off like the coward he is," admitted Renault. "He's probably somewhere in the city by now, hiding out."

"Well, we need him to sign the command of the Protectors back over," said Naz. "Otherwise, King Lakton will continue to be powerless."

"Perhaps," said Jemima, coming in beside him. He beamed at her in happiness. "We can create a new Protector force. One that has a completely new governance system in place to ensure that an Uprising movement can never rise up again."

"I'd agree with that," grunted Octavia.

Naz looked at him in concern. His shoulder looked brutalised, and although Geetie had managed to get Renault's sword out, he was unsure if Octavia would ever be able to fight again.

"An order," said Lekt, approaching them. "That requires the votes of all council members to ultimately give command. No singular voice, such as my father's or Balnather's, can ever have sole control of the new Protectors." He turned to his father who looked at them all sadly.

"So be it," croaked Lakton. "Balnather can keep the old Protectors." He turned to Octavia. "My old friend," he began. "Would you command them? Would you become the Chief once more?"

"Nay, my Lord," replied Octavia, looking at his shoulder wincing from the pain. "My time is over." He looked to Naz. "I think younger blood is needed."

"So be it," said Lakton. Suddenly he stood up straight and appeared mighty once more. "Naz, I invite you to become the first Chief of the New Protectors of Harleland."

Naz breathed in shock. *Him?* He gazed at Lakton. "My Lord," he breathed. "It would be my honour."

Drew approached Octavia now and withdrew a bag from within his coat. Naz gazed in wonder as he took out what seemed to be a glowing green leaf from within the bag. He heard Drew whisper a word.

Devine.

Suddenly, Octavia's shoulder began to heal. The former Chief gazed in wonder as his broken and bloody shoulder became healed by whatever strange spell Drew had cast.

"Those are not the same runes I gave you," said Lakton in amazement. "You are certainly full of surprises, Saran."

Suddenly, a great cry went up from outside. All present, except for the injured, rushed outside and looked. Horror swept through Naz. The Crownlands were coming. No, not just any Herk army. A great battalion. A sea of Herks. The biggest army any of them had ever seen. He stared at Prince Lekt in shock as he came in beside Naz.

"What do we do?" the Prince asked. "After everything we have done, wrestling back control of Boron Nigh, we can't let things end like this."

"They won't," said Naz with conviction. "We'll make one final stand." He looked at his charges. He was in charge of them now, and it was his duty to protect them and all within this Kingdom.

"Sir," said Drew, approaching him. "I think I need to handle this."

"Will you use the magic leaves again?" he asked. "Are those your runes that I have heard about?"

Drew picked out one of his stone, purple runes and whispered:

Height.

He began to levitate and floated high above the city streets. Naz stared in amazement as he saw Drew take one of his green, leaf runes. Suddenly, a great shield, like a bubble Naz thought, surrounded the entirety of Boron Nigh. The army of the Crownlands stopped their march. Drew took out another stone rune suddenly his voice boomed throughout the world, heard even by the Crownland army before the city.

"This city is protected," he boomed. "Surrender now."

Suddenly, Naz spotted something unbelievable. He had to rub his eyes and shake his head to ensure he was not hallucinating. There were white flags being raised by the army below. He looked at Prince Lekt, and then to King Lakton.

"So I was wrong," said Lakton. "Ker Gorûn must be heeded." He turned to Lekt. "I made mistakes in my life my son. I know you will too, in a bid to protect your Kingdom. But a wise King must know when to admit their mistakes." He sighed. "Your first act as King must be to meet with Shârvous and arrange a truce."

"But father," said Lekt in confusion. "You are still the King?"

Lakton stumbled and coughed. Lekt caught him and looked at his father in alarm. The King took off his crown and gave it to his son.

"This is where we part…" he whispered.

To the amazement of all present, a soft breeze came through and the King appeared to disintegrate into dust, the wind blowing it away. Naz looked upon the distraught Prince.

"You are our King now," he said. "And I pledge my allegiance to you."

"No," said Lekt. "Pledge your allegiance not to me, but to the people."

He had determination in his eyes. Lekt put his father's crown upon his head and from that moment on he became known as King Lekt the Second, and he descended from Palace Rock with Naz, his Chief of the New Protectors, and Drew, who floated down to meet them at the main gates of the city.

"Whatever happens now," breathed the King. "Will be remembered for the next several ages."

Flanked by Drew and Naz, King Lekt strode confidently out the gate and came face to face with the one man who had ordered wave after wave of Herk attacks on Harleland. The singular biggest enemy Harleland had faced since the Independence Wars over a century ago. Waiting for them, sitting on a great brown steed, was Duke Shârvous.

Green Tree

Chapter Twenty-Nine

Drew stared at him. This was the man he hated with the strongest resolve. He thought back. He sat in the orphanage, with Hermit and Kora, as they prepared to leave for their cadet camp at Bunglemere Heights the next day.

"If you came face to face with Shârvous," Hermit asked. "What would you do?"

"And *don't* say you'd immediately start striking him with your sword," Kora said. "Remember, he's a bit more of an opponent than Hermit is."

"Hey!" said Hermit. "I'll have you know, I beat Drew just last week."

"That is true," said Drew awkwardly, looking at Kora, quickly drinking in how pretty she looked, and then looking away again before she could see. "I think it would depend on the circumstances of our meeting."

Hermit shrugged. "So be it," he said, as he chowed down a chicken drumstick.

"Some of Mrs Crakanthorpe's finest!" said Phil, coming up behind Hermit unannounced.

Hermit almost choked. "Phil!" he said. "You gotta give me some warning!"

Phil shrugged. "I'm just glad it's not slop tonight."

"Don't let Julia hear you say that," said Kora. "Or that's all you'll get!"

"Oh, yeah, whatever," said Phil. "Anyways you three, make sure ya's all eat up! Gotta be nice and strong for cadet camp tomorrow."

"I'm already nice and strong," said Hermit, causing Drew and Kora to laugh.

Drew sighed. "If I came face to face with Shârvous," he continued. "I'd ask him… why has he done this? And is he happy?"

"Well?" Drew asked again, back in the present, while King Lekt and Naz stood beside him. "Was it all worth it?"

Shârvous looked silently at Drew. Then he dismounted his horse and removed his helmet. He was wearing the same style of armour any ordinary Herk would wear, and he seemed to have long black hair, tied neatly in a ponytail. But his face certainly did not speak of war. It was… fair. He had a neatly shaved beard and blue eyes, and was all round nothing like Drew had imagined him. Even more strange was the smile on his face.

"Well, if you are anything like your uncle, then I shall be glad to be your acquaintance," the Duke of the Crownlands said, holding out his hand to Drew.

He shook it. Shârvous turned then to Lekt and Naz.

"Condolences, my King," he said. "I respected Lakton for his convictions, although I am glad that we now have new leadership."

"I come here to negotiate a truce," declared Lekt. "It is time to end this war."

"Of course," replied Shârvous. "But that of course means terms that benefit the both of us."

"I am prepared for that," said Lekt.

"And I see that Octavia is no longer your Chief?" Shârvous asked, looking at Naz.

"Octavia has retired," Naz declared.

"Very well," said Shârvous. "Send him my best wishes."

Drew noticed, amongst the Herks behind the Duke, was Captain Crysthan. They nodded at each other. An exchange of genuine respect. But it did not last long, for now, Drew gazed upon Shârvous in spite. There was something off putting about this individual. He felt stronger than ever the same level of hatred toward the Crownlands he had felt before leaving for Hoonth. A hatred that burned into his very soul. And right now, being before the man himself, Drew felt the most unhinged he had ever felt.

You could kill him, said the voice. And Drew was almost inclined to agree, until he heard another voice. One that was familiar, but that had not spoken to him before the same way the original voice had.

You no longer control him.

Drew gasped. It was the voice of Lazarka, protecting him from whatever evil was inside his head. He shook himself. Indeed, it appeared that the Life Runes provided some sort of counterbalance to the Shadow Runes. Quickly as that, both voices seemed to vanish, and Drew was once more aware of reality.

"I shall agree to your truce," declared Shârvous. "The fighting shall cease! But in exchange, Harleland must recognise the Crownlands' status as a Sovereign Grand Dutchy once again, like we were before my ancestors pledged vassalage to Merthru."

Lekt bristled but appeared ready to accept the terms. Suddenly, a shout came from behind them. Drew turned and saw Balnather standing at the gate, General Mortimus and Sergeant Elias by his side.

"See!" crowed the former Uprising Inquisitor. "The Royals are selling us out to the Crownlands!"

Shârvous laughed. "And who is this pathetic little creature?" he asked.

Balnather gazed at him in anger. "I am King Balnather!" he screamed. "Great Leader of Harleland!" He turned back to Elias and Mortimus, only to give a cry of fear. "Where is the army?" he asked. "Why is there no army of Protectors?"

"Those who remained refused to follow us, sir," replied Mortimus.

Balnather looked around in terror. As he went to run, Naz grabbed him by the scruff of the neck and threw him down before King Lekt. The King looked down upon the traitor in anger. Balnather now grovelled at his feet. Drew watched on in satisfaction.

"I offer you mercy," declared Lekt. "However, you will spend the remainder of your life in prison for high treason."

"No!" he screamed, and he ran, but unfortunately for Balnather it was right into Shârvous who did not hesitate to quickly cut off his head. It rolled back towards Drew, who stared at it with a feeling of victory.

"As I was saying," continued Lekt. "I accept your terms. Let us move forward in peace."

"So be it," agreed Shârvous.

The Crownland Duke caught Drew's eye as he shook King Lekt's hand and winked at him.

Drew quickly looked away and turned towards Naz, while Mortimus and Elias surrendered themselves to a group of Protectors, who swiftly took them to await trial. Naz laughed.

"It all worked out, huh?" he asked.

"I guess so," replied Drew, a feeling of unease stirring inside him. "It all worked out."

Epilogue

Rain poured upon the smooth, dark stone roof of the Black Fortress. Even deep within the great castle, the sound of the storm outside could be faintly heard. Candles flickered on the dark walls, giving off a dull light. Herks slowly patrolled the corridors, marching up and down, ensuring the security of their Lord's residence. The uneasy peace was broken as a pair of senior looking Herk soldiers dragged a ragged figure across the ground toward a great pair of spruce doors. The prisoner gasped in pain as he was sharply jerked onto his knees by his captors. As they came to a halt, a silence fell again, the only sound audible being that of the guards marching up and down the halls. The doors began to open, and out stepped a tall man in white robes, a great black staff in his right hand.

"Lord Zebtion," began one of the Herk captors. "We have the *failure* Captain Crysthan, as per the good Duke's orders."

"Excellent," replied Zebtion. "Lord Shârvous awaits you now."

He eyed Crysthan menacingly. Crysthan met Zebtion's gaze. This crackpot old wizard did not scare him. He had always been suspicious of this wily old sorcerer and had long since suspected him of attempting to undermine Shârvous.

"My Lord!" called Zebtion, walking back through the doors and into a well-lit great hall. "I present to you, Crysthan the Traitor!"

Upon his throne, Duke Shârvous rose and eyed Crysthan with contempt. However, when he spoke, he sounded more… disappointed than angry.

"You have failed me," Shârvous said calmly.

"I'm sorry, my Lord," replied Crysthan. "But this Andrew Saran overpowered me. He carries something. A great power. I don't know how to explain it."

"We had that petty Kingdom on the ropes," replied Shârvous, a violent look coming over him. "This ceasefire has ruined my existing plans! You should have killed Saran in Wilder Forest when you had the chance." The Lord of the Crownlands calmed down, and he spoke again in a soft yet much more menacing voice. "Plans change however, and we must now use this truce to bide our time."

"It was as I foresaw," said a new voice.

From the shadows stepped Count Michael. He exchanged a look with Zebtion, who bowed to his superior.

"My nephew carries the Shadow Runes," continued Michael, a grave expression on his face. "And I have no doubt that the great spell he cast yesterday at Boron Nigh that created an impenetrable shield was a power gifted by the Life Runes."

"So he has two sets of runes now," said Shârvous thoughtfully. "We must pick up the pace! We cannot be caught off guard again!" He looked accusingly at Michael. "Your nephew is proving quite the roadblock, Count Michael."

There seemed to be a flicker of anger in Michael's eyes at Shârvous' words, but he recomposed himself. He looked over at Zebtion.

"Zebtion has located the Weather Runes," said the Count.

"That is right my Lord," replied Zebtion.

"Very good," said Shârvous.

"It is vital we prevent him from obtaining the other runes," continued Michael, Crysthan noticing a flicker of unease in the Count's facial expressions.

Zebtion strode over to the Duke and whispered something in his ear. Shârvous nodded. He stood and looked upon Crysthan. "Captain, I am a generous man. And I give my charges second chances." He approached Crysthan. "Rise, my friend."

Crysthan did as he was told, a feeling of unease stirring within him.

"Andrew Saran has presented himself as a threat to my plans," explained Shârvous. "We are now forced to change tact. Captain Crysthan – you will go to Boron Nigh and befriend him. If the Weather Runes are where Zebtion says they are, it will not take Saran long to find them. And once he has them – that is when you shall strike."

Crysthan nodded his understanding.

"This is your second and final chance Captain Crysthan," said Shârvous. "Fail me again, and you shall be subject to a fate worse than death."

Fear flickered through Crysthan as he heard Zebtion snicker, while Count Michael stood next to Shârvous with an unreadable expression on his face.

"Succeed however – and you shall forever be known as the man who obtained three sets of runes for *me*," the Duke continued.

"All hail Shârvous, true Lord and Master of the Runes," crooned Zebtion in a horrible, whiny and obedient tone.

Duke Shârvous smiled. Crysthan knew it. This ceasefire was a ploy to buy the Crownlands time – and soon, the runes would be in the possession of the Lord of the Crownlands.

About The Author

M.L. Hendry

Matthew Hendry first began writing stories as a child, slowly making them less embarassing over time. In 2012, he began writing a story with help from his brother Jordan. Several years later, Matthew decided to use that tale as a basis for his first novel *Great Tower*, which he published in 2024.

Outside of writing, Matthew is a keen NRL fan, spending several years of his life banging his head against a wall watching his beloved Canterbury Bulldogs.

He enjoys travelling, having been to several European destinations with a strong desire to explore more.

Green Tree

Books In This Series

The Great Tower Saga

Andrew Saran is destined to master the mysterious runes, going on dangerous quests and meeting new and interesting people as he tries to save Harleland from Duke Shârvous...

Great Tower

In the Kingdom of Harleland, a young orphan is tasked with a dangerous quest to save his land from a destructive civil war.

Blue Ocean (Coming Soon!)

Far over the Sea of Many Currents, a new rebellion grows as Drew, Josh and Tenebrae set out on their next adventure to find the legendary Ocean Sapphire.